DEMON HUNTRESS

DEMON HUNT
BOOK ONE

MILLY TAIDEN

ABOUT THE BOOK

Demon hunter Cassandra Merewen is on the trail of a demon conspiracy. **She's the best of the best, and nothing will get in the way of her completing the job. Well, except for two gorgeous wolf shifters who she can't get out of her mind.** But she's her own lone wolf who will never let her heart be entangled. Her life's mission won't allow it.

Co-alphas Slade Reynolds and Flash Winterpaw are about as dysfunctional as friends can be. Slade has lost everyone he's ever loved, and Flash has issues no doctor can cure. Their only hope is to find their one true mate who supposedly will complete them. **And once they lay their eyes**

on Cassandra, they know there's no other woman for them.

But what can they do when said mate refuses to open her heart to them? **How can a couple of clueless bachelors romance a woman who knows what she wants out of life, and it's not them?**

DEMON HUNTRESS

DEMON HUNT 1

NEW YORK TIMES and USA TODAY BESTSELLING

AUTHOR

MILLY TAIDEN

This book is a work of fiction. The names, characters, places, and incidents are fictitious or have been used fictitiously, and are not to be construed as real in any way. Any resemblance to persons, living or dead, actual events, locales, or organizations is entirely coincidental.

Published By
Latin Goddess Press
Winter Springs, FL 32708
http://millytaiden.com
Demon Huntress

 Created with Vellum

—*For my badass readers.*

You Rock!

CHAPTER I

CASSANDRA

She pulled her chalk out of her pocket, making quick work of drawing the penta-gram along the sidewalk. She drew up the wall of the building and down over the concrete to make sure each line touched, bringing it all together.

Mere seconds ago, she caught sight of the demon stepping into the store. You wouldn't have guessed what he was with his stern face, brown hair going gray, and expensive suit.

But Cassandra had followed him for hours, and no one could say she wasn't invested in her work because she had followed the demon to the Bronx, for heaven's sake.

She closed her eyes as she bent down and

placed her fingers on the ground. She pushed her power into it, watching it shine for a second before it stopped. She stared at it, feeling the power on the chalk. Once the demon entered the pentagram, he couldn't leave. She would get the answers she needed from him.

The door to the shop opened, and she stepped away like she was a normal person passing by until she heard the man hissing out with a screech. She smiled, knowing she had him. It was taking candy from a child.

She looked over her shoulder, taking him in. He looked around, confused until his eyes landed on her. They narrowed, and he scowled at her, enraged. He knew who she was, and he knew what she'd done.

"Interesting." She smirked, turning to him. "I honestly thought it would take a little more to slow you down, but I guess you're just a lower-level demon, aren't you?"

"What do you want?" He snarled at her, unable to step over the chalk. She could see he wanted to.

She crossed her arms, needing to work this in her favor. "I have a few questions I would like answered. It's a very painless process, I promise."

"And why would I help you?" he growled back,

snapping his teeth. He glanced around at the chalk before his eyes came back up to her. "I'm not helping a demon hunter."

She pulled her chalk back out, rolling it in her palm. "I can make your cage even smaller if you would like. Maybe you'll be up for talking then."

"I'm not telling you anything," he growled.

She made a sad face, tilting her head slightly. "That's a pity because I was up for bargaining. You know, *give me a name, and I'll let you live* kind of thing. But if you're not down for that kind of an agreement, I guess I could just let you stand here forever."

Everything she was saying was a lie, but he didn't know that. She never gave anything away on her face. "Guess I'll just have to kill you instead."

"What makes you think I have any information you want? You're going to kill an innocent person before you even know if they have anything you need?" He laughed. "Is that how you demon hunters work now?"

She laughed and rolled her eyes. She shook her head, glaring at him. "You're hardly innocent, so don't try. And I happen to know you are involved in a vast demonic conspiracy. I have my way of finding out what I need. Give me a name, and maybe I'll be nice tonight. I'm feeling giving."

He studied her for a moment, his mind churning. He had no way out, and honestly, she was his only answer.

"If I give you a name, you'll let me walk?" He glanced at the chalk. "You'll remove this so I can leave?"

"God's honor." She smirked, batting her eyes. That wasn't entirely her plan. He would be leaving, but not the way he was thinking. He wasn't leaving alive.

He took a deep breath before he sighed. He rubbed his eyes and squeezed his hands into fists. He looked at her, and his face fell. "Phar-scape ..." Suddenly, his entire body tensed, and he screamed. She jumped back, startled. She covered her ears, stunned by the intensity of his volume.

His jaw unhinged, a red haze filled his mouth, and his body started to glow orange. Her eyes widened as she realized he was burning from the inside out.

Smoke rose as his body continued to blister, and he tumbled to his knees, snapped, and crumbled to the ground. Her magic tingled, feeling another demon's presence fill the area. It made her hair stand up.

She scanned the alleyway and the rooftop seeing nothing. Someone higher on the evil chain didn't want this man saying anything. Quickly, his insides turned to ash, and the rest of him disintegrated. She frowned, wishing she had gotten more out of him first.

She curled her hands into tight fists and sighed. Damn it. She pinched the bridge of her nose, tired. She needed sleep, but she needed answers more.

She arrived back at her hotel room, frustrated. She grabbed her laptop off her bed and swung into the nearest chair. She flipped it open and typed in the name the demon gave her.

She scanned the different articles and newspaper clippings, finding it was a company on the verge of being worth a billion dollars thanks to the rollout of Torpor, a drug promised to relieve suffering from depression. It was supposed to be the newest and best thing for people who struggled with it.

The articles didn't give her much, leaving her with more questions than answers. What did demons want with antidepressants? She wasn't seeing any connection that would make sense.

She didn't like mysteries, and she knew someone who could figure the answer out faster than she ever would. He could break in where she needed him to and get her the keys she was looking for.

She flipped her phone out, dialing up Greg's number. He answered on the third ring. "Cassandra, long time no call." He spoke in a charming, teasing tone.

She adjusted her phone, opening another article. "Hey, Greg. I have a name for you to look up if you have a spare moment."

He softly chuckled. "Aww, can't even spare me five seconds to talk? You want to go straight to business?"

She scowled, and he laughed on the other end. "I'm kidding. What's the name?"

She rolled her eyes. She and Greg had worked together long enough that he knew she was always business. She rarely opened up to people, and that included him. He only knew what she wanted him to know about her.

"Phar-Scape. Can you find your way into their

database and get me anything? I see they have an antidepressant they're marketing, but I'm not seeing how this links. What would demons need with that?"

She heard him typing at his keyboard, and she looked at her breakfast which she hardly ate because she had to leave her room early enough to catch the demon.

She hadn't eaten since this morning, and it was well past ten p.m. now. She was used to pushing her hunger away when she was focused. She had to if she wanted to be one of the best.

Greg grumbled before he sighed. "They have really sound security, it looks like I can't access their database, but I can get into their human resources system if that's any help."

She thought about it, biting her nail for a moment. She nodded. She remembered reading that they were hiring. "Yes, put me down as one of the new hires in their assistant pool. I can get inside and find out what we need from there. I can figure out what demons are doing with a pharmaceutical company because I'm guessing nothing good."

She heard Greg typing once more. "You would probably be correct. Are you sure we shouldn't bring in other hunters? This is a big deal, and you might could use the extra backup."

She scowled, irritated. She hated when Greg brought up having another person working with her. She preferred to work alone, and he knew this. She *needed* to work alone. It was better that way. She could focus her entire attention on the job, and it would get done correctly.

"No," she said, shaking her head. "I don't need anyone else on this case with me. Just add me to the pool, and I'll get everything from the inside."

"Cassandra." She noted the shift in his tone, the kind he used when he was worried. She didn't like it. She didn't want to hear him go on about her needing help.

She frowned. "Do we want a repeat of the last time I worked with someone? Because I don't think we do."

Greg fell silent, and she knew she had won. But she didn't win, though, because she didn't want to think about her past. She didn't want to think at all.

She hung up without saying anything and sighed, tossing her phone aside. She shook her head, not wanting to think about her concerns.

She had no one to share her feelings or thoughts with. But that was how she wanted it, needed it.

She frowned, realizing just how lonely she was, but it was how it had to be. And after a while, she thought she would come to terms with it, but there were days she struggled. Today was one of them.

CHAPTER 2

FLASH

Flash was going to see this mission through, and he didn't care how many rules he had to break in the process. He knew the world wasn't black and white, and sometimes, he had to step over people to do what needed to be done.

He glanced at the palatial estate that he intended to break into. It belonged to Henry Crenshaw's accountant, and he'd been working too hard to wait for a chance to get inside. He couldn't wait anymore.

He'd been trying to get dirt on the Phar-scape ever since he was freed not that long ago. Thinking about where he was standing only made him angry. They deserved to all burn to the ground for what they did.

He still had nightmares from everything that he had to endure while they held him captive for years. God, he'd lost track of all the needles and the drugs they forced into his body. He was always weak, vomiting, and his body convulsed against everything, but there was nothing he could do. He was always in a state of absence. Until that one night when he escaped, and everything changed.

He'd been captured by Phar-Scape when he was nineteen. He didn't remember how he got himself into the situation, but he had, and for years they did horrible experiments on him.

He remembered the cold sweats and the body shakes that started deep in his bones. He had constant headaches, and his vision never seemed right. Everything hurt all the time.

There were only slivers of his youth that he remembered. Otherwise, most of it was erased so they could create the perfect killer. Their plan would have worked if he hadn't been freed by Slade, who was a childhood friend who never gave up on him.

If Slade knew he was here right now, he'd

probably beat the crap out of him for being so irrational. He couldn't help it, though. After being held for so long, his anger got the better of him.

He had tried to learn to keep it together, but it was one of his weak spots. He couldn't. He was like a broken record, and little by little, more of his pieces came together, but there were plenty of pieces that didn't fit, and every once in a while, he broke it apart to start all over again.

He shook his head and glanced over the garden. He almost forgot he was on a mission. He needed to stay out of his head. It was never wired right, and it was always better when he worked. He didn't have to think. He could always ask for forgiveness later.

Sure, Slade would be angry, but he would get over it. He always did. Slade understood him, and as co-alpha, Slade knew he ran things differently. It was how they got along so well. It was also how they fought. He was the hot-headed one, and Slade was the thinker.

He snuck around the side of the garden and made his way through a broken board, slipping to the other side. The garden was full of plants and flowers and the smell of perfume. He scrunched his nose and froze when he caught another scent. One that he knew really well.

He scowled and then heard the soft footsteps behind him coming around the garden just like he had.

He turned, looking at Slade as he slipped through the board. Slade was a tall man with deep red hair cut short at the moment. Flash's bright blue eyes stopped on him, and he could smell that he had recently had a cigar, one of his nasty habits.

Flash scowled, crossing his arms. "Couldn't leave me alone for five minutes, could you?"

Slade scowled back at him. "You didn't make it hard to find you. If you really didn't want to be found, you should have tried to be sneakier."

He sighed. He should have known he was there to tell him to go back home. He didn't approve of everything that he did. It wasn't that Slade and he got along perfectly because they didn't.

Before he was kidnapped, they never saw eye to eye. They were rivals and hated each other. After a female dumped both of them, they learned that maybe fighting wasn't the best idea.

"How did you even know I would be here?" he asked, irritated. He thought he had been pretty careful, but then again, this was Slade. He knew him well.

He raised an eyebrow and tilted his head to the side. "Flash, it isn't like it's hard to put two and two together. I know you hold a vendetta for everything they have done and that you were watching the accountant. I decided to follow you to make sure nothing happened."

He crossed his arms, not wanting to hear him tell him how this was a bad idea. He didn't care. He had wanted to do this for months, and Slade wasn't going to change that. "Don't try to stop me, Slade. I'm doing this." He could have gone over all the reasons why but he didn't.

Slade pulled both of his hands up, nodding. "I'm not going to. I'm here to help. Let's nail this bastard. Make them pay for everything."

Slade gave him a chuckle before he walked closer. "So, what's the plan?"

He watched as he stretched his arms, ready to do whatever he wanted. He couldn't help but be grateful. After everything, he wanted to make those people pay for what they did to him.

They were up to something, and he wanted to ensure that no one ever had to go through what he went through. Whatever they were planning, he was going to put a stop to it.

He looked over the garden and then at the large house that the accountant lived in. It was a two-story home with an entire security team and a large gate which they had already passed.

"The accountant is out on vacation, but all of his staff are still here. Avoid hurting the domestic servants, but most of the security are workers from the business. They get shifted around, so I can tell you their hands aren't clean."

Which was a nice way of saying if they ended up killing a few, he wouldn't have nightmares about it later. They weren't innocent. It wasn't any extra stress on him whether they were alive or dead.

He moved first, stepping around the garden and headed for the back entrance. Slade was right behind him, following his lead. They watched as a maid walked through the kitchen into the long hallway. He slipped the door open, and they slid inside.

They headed down another hallway when a door beside Slade opened. They both turned, and Slade grabbed the man around the throat and twisted. The guard's neck snapped, and Slade caught him before he could fall.

He dragged the man back into the room, shutting the door all within a minute. Slade sighed and gave Flash a nod to move forward.

They took out three more guards before they made it to the second floor, where they finally found the office. Flash threw himself into the chair and opened the computer. He looked at Slade, who was keeping watch in the hallway.

They had about five minutes before they needed to get out. If the security was good, that was the amount of time he was giving himself. That, and someone was bound to find one of the bodies they had left.

He broke into the initial passcodes and tried to flip through the files, then another hack popped up. He scowled, irritated.

Suddenly, the software went berserk, and he realized that either magic or some demonic shit had been tied to the technology. He had no idea how that worked, but it wasn't the first time he'd experienced this kind of weird crap with Phar-Scape.

"Fuck," he said as the room started to shake. Shit. Shit. SHIT.

Slade's eyes widened. "What did you do?"

First, a pen and then a book floated from the desk. Great. A poltergeist. Just what they needed. Things flew around the room, smacking him.

Ducking as the stapler tried to slam into his head, he slid the flash drive into the computer. Slade cursed, avoiding a chair zipping across the room.

Flash dodged being hit by a plant, and his anger grew hotter by the second. Who the fuck puts this on their computer? Well, someone who knew there was a possibility of being hacked, that's who.

Damn it. How had he not seen this? How had he not thought about it? He should have. He knew better.

"Flash," Slade growled, snapping his attention toward him. "Is it downloaded? We need to get out. NOW!"

He glanced at the computer, feeling the room shift once more. Heavier objects were now moving. Fuck. This was just great.

The files were downloaded, and he yanked the flash drive free, moving out of the way as the filing cabinet slammed into the desk, missing him by inches.

He kicked it, cursing several times. Again, who plans for this shit?

"Flash." Slade grabbed his shoulder, turning him. "Get your head out of your ass. We need to go."

An invisible tornado filled the room, papers flying and the lights flickering. With Slade, they burst out of the office into the hallway. Guards yelled as they raced down the staircase, breaking the railing as they went. Bullets whizzed by their heads.

He could feel Slade's eyes on him as they piled into his car. "The fuck was that? You let your anger rule you, and you stalled. We could've gotten pinned in there because you can't control your anger."

He frowned, clenching his jaw. He wanted to argue, but what could he say? Slade had a point.

"Your inability to handle your anger is going to get us into a situation we can't get out of. You need to get it under control. Now."

He remained silent.

"And you better pray that whatever the fuck was back there stays because, I swear to god, if you unleashed something on us, I'll fucking hurt you."

"It won't," he grumbled, ready for the drive to

be over. He wasn't a five-year-old. He was a grown-ass man who could make his own decisions. He made a mistake, and he was ready to move on.

"You better be right." Slade stepped on the gas, silencing the argument.

He was wrong. Once they were home, they realized the demonic fucker that he unleashed at the house had ventured home with them.

Pissed, Slade stood with his arms crossed in the kitchen, glaring as the lights flickered. Flash sat in the other room, trying to ignore the flying objects, but it was impossible. He also knew it wasn't going to go away.

"We need to call someone," Slade said, stepping into the living room. His anger had morphed into exhaustion.

"Who?"

"A demon hunter."

"Seriously?" he grumbled.

"Yes, because this isn't stopping."

A chair flew by, slamming into the wall. Slade waved a hand, and Flashed frowned. Maybe he had a point. Again.

"Fine." He pulled himself up. "Do you know anyone?"

Slade nodded, and it didn't surprise him. His friend knew a wide range of people who could help him with different situations. It came in handy in moments like this.

"I'll make the call." Slade turned and slipped down the hallway. Flash flinched as the lights went out and sighed. All right, maybe he fucked up.

CHAPTER 3

CASSANDRA

After being home and planning for several days, Cassandra had the next part of her mission ready to activate. She always enjoyed picking her outfit for the next day, especially when it was the beginning of an assignment. It helped her settle into the mood, the personality, and the mask of the character she was setting out to portray. When it came to blending into Phar-Scape, she wanted to go with a sleek pants suit that fit the lean muscles of her frame.

She was wandering through her vast closet when her phone on the bedside table rang. She had stripped down to her underwear and bra, which were a durable lace getup that she often wore for potential suitors. It made her feel undeniably sexy, so she wore it around the house, catching glimpses of herself and fawning the way a proper lover would.

Cassandra sighed and answered. "Don't tell me something is wrong this late?" she snapped.

She put the phone on speaker as she wandered back into her closet, staring at the vast wheel of shades and fabrics she had accumulated over years of climbing the huntress ladder.

"I've got a favor to ask of you," he began. "There's a friend of mine who's got a poltergeist harassing him, and I think your intervention would do him some good."

She had both hands on her hips when the request slithered through her like a garden snake. She shot back at the phone, nearly hissing through the narrow space between her lips.

"You must be joking," she replied. "Greg, that kind of shit is lightyears below my pay grade. You, of all people, should know that."

"You owe me, Cass," he said, sounding more confident than usual. "Remember when I helped you do your taxes? You would have been lost without me."

Cassandra paused at the audacity, half-offended and half-impressed by his bold assertion.

She picked up a violet long-sleeve T-shirt and leather pants that made her ass look like a baby pumpkin.

"You have really grown some balls at the most inconvenient time, Greggy boy," she remarked, laying the clothes out on the bed.

Greg remained silent, not taking the bait of her bullying statement for once. She let out a long, heaving sigh that made her lips vibrate before speaking.

"I have to sleep, Greg," she said, attempting to keep her tone even and cordial. "This case with Phar-Scape is looking pretty fucking big."

Greg replied hastily as if the words were vomit pouring out of his mouth. "You have to do it tonight, Cass," he said. "This one is pretty aggressive, and it needs your expert eye."

The compliment was like getting your ass smacked by a sexy stranger; at first, you recoil, and then, another part of you is drawn to the delinquency of the act. She let out another sigh blended with a grunt, then asked him to give her the address.

Cassandra wore a comfortable and agile set of clothing that had become her signature go-to outfit. When it came right down to it, Cassandra wasn't fond of physically fighting demons at all. Even though she was a human with special abilities, she was still human and bled and died like every other human.

So her skills and technique relied utterly on stealth and discrete movements. She would stalk her subjects until they were secluded enough for her to either capture or destroy them in what she hoped would be a single fatal blow. Getting into a skirmish with any of them was her last option, if it was an option at all.

She had been trained in martial arts and military techniques of infiltration and extraction. It was crucial to be able to track a demon without them noticing, and Cassandra was an absolute specialist at it. So it was slightly insulting when Greg had asked her to get rid of a poltergeist for some friend of his. It was far less interesting to Cassandra than the demon hunting she was used to, almost amateurish and suited for people just getting started in the demon hunting game. But he had helped her with something that she had coerced him into doing.

She brooded to herself as she drove through New York in the dead of night, the lights of the city blasting by like streaks of meteorites. She followed the instructions on her GPS into the dim world of the boondocks outside the city and away from the gleam of life.

"Where the fuck are you taking me, Greg?" she whispered to herself.

Cassandra drove along a dirt trail, swallowed in darkness, until she came across a rugged but upscale-looking home. It was entirely made of varnished cherry wood and looked like something a millionaire would choose to seclude themselves away from humanity

It wasn't the classic distressed cottage type. Whoever was in there obviously had money to get something so lavish and specifically built for them. She scoffed to herself about the boldness of some rich bastards calling her in the middle of the night to get rid of some pithy poltergeist.

But as she got out of the car and walked up to the house, a wash of lights popping along the driveway like a catwalk, she realized the entity wasn't as weak as she had assumed.

The energy moved through the tips of her fingers like the sensation of pins and needles, then became thick and bulky as it traveled up her limbs and settled in her chest. It was a sensation she was used to and had cultivated since starting her demon hunting career, but something about the poltergeist made her uneasy.

She approached the house with her regular confidence, adjusted her hair into a secure pony-tail, then knocked on the door.

She heard a deep, bellowing voice call out to her before the door swung open to reveal a sight that nearly knocked her on her ass.

A man nearly twice her size answered the door in only boxer shorts, showcasing a bulge that Cassandra figured he had difficulty hiding. The muscles of his arms and shoulders were streaked with lovely webs of veins, pulsing and straining as he shoved the door open and slammed it against the wall inside.

She had to squeeze her thighs together at the sight of him and bite her lip, nearly piercing the supple skin.

The man sported disheveled, medium-length black hair with hazel eyes that looked like a painter's dream. She felt her body throbbing for him for the few seconds that he didn't speak.

"Who the fuck are you?" he snarled at her.

Cassandra cocked an eyebrow nonchalantly. "You weren't expecting someone?"

He looked her up and down without any hesitation or subtly. His pink tongue even emerged from his lips as those eyes traced the curve of her ass, the thick solidity of her hips and waist. Her breasts were hidden, of course, but the bra she was wearing outlined them like a flawless silhouette under the glow of the porch lamp.

"Why on earth would a gorgeous piece of ass like you show up on my doorstep?"

His arms dropped down from the doorframe and crossed, then he leaned against the door itself. Cassandra gave him a deep scowl that made her feel like there would be a permanent indentation on her forehead.

"You really have given first impressions a bad name, haven't you?" she said, looking a bit amused.

The man opened his mouth to say something that was likely just as offensive, but something crashed into the side of his face to ruin his concentration. Cassandra had to cover her mouth for a second to keep from showing how amused she was.

It looked like a dark purple vase had been flung from the living room to the front door by the very entity she had been called to dispel.

"Fucking hell!" the man screamed.

"I'm the demon hunter you hired," Cassandra said icily, stepping inside with her bag of tricks. "The woman who is going to get rid of the thing that just handed you your ass."

The man rubbed at his head like a child, gazing at the broken pieces of the ceramic vase on the floor. Before he could speak again, another gem of a man came tumbling downstairs, but he was wearing sweatpants and a T-shirt.

He, too, was looking like a slice of heaven, and Cassandra once again had to get herself together by making her expression overly stoic. The urge to groan out loud was overwhelming.

"I'm so sorry," the new man said.

Once he came down the stairs, he took hold of Cassandra's hand, shaking it like a shark would shake a piece of fish.

"Forgive my friend's behavior. Cordiality isn't his specialty."

The man who shook her hand had a similar build as the one without his shirt, with bulging muscles for days that almost looked prosthetic. He had blazing red hair cut neatly and a smooth face that looked like it had been recently shaved. His eyes were bright sky blue that sent shivers down her spine, all the way to her sex between her legs.

"My name is Slade," the red-headed man said. "And this ass is Flash."

Flash was still rubbing his head as if the collision had injured him. Slade growled at him as he let Cassandra's hand go.

"No offense taken," she replied lightheartedly. "I am often mistaken for a common strumpet as opposed to the expert demon hunter I am."

The two men had no idea had to take her attempt at dry, sarcastic wit. It was something very few people in her life understood, and she wasn't completely surprised that it had utterly failed with the two hotties she had just encountered. She chuckled to herself, then placed the bag down.

"That's what they call a joke," she said, smoothing her shirt.

Slade was the first to smile while Flash picked up the pieces of the vase off the floor. The entire time, despite being distracted by the subject's attractiveness, Cassandra sensed the energy moving around, and it was even more agitated by her presence.

"So," she began, looking around the decadent house. "I'm assuming neither of you has worked with a demon hunter before, correct?"

They stood like puppets staring at her, shaking their heads simultaneously. The scene was so ridiculous that her lips curved into a devilish smile.

"I have certain methods that have proven successful in the past," she began. "If you could show me to the room with the most activity, I can get started."

"No problem," Slade said, giving her a warm smile.

Cassandra had to look away from his stone-carved jaw to keep herself together. It had been so long since she had been this attracted to anyone, much less two people at the same time. The attraction was palpable inside her chest and between her thighs, almost as strong as the entity she felt swirling around the house.

It was nearly enough for her to forsake her duty and rip her clothes off in front of them. One or the other could take her. She wouldn't care. Even both, if she was so lucky.

"What a delicious notion," she murmured to herself.

Slade led her up the carpeted stairs, and she did her best to stay focused.

SLADE

Slade had nearly stumbled down the stairs when he caught the scent of the demon hunter standing at their door. The woman was the definition of elegance, sporting tight-fitting clothing and a ponytail that pulled back every string of hair that sat on top of her head. She was a fair distance away, but her ice-blue eyes stood out in the dark like fireflies.

She smelled of enchanting vanilla, lemon, and sage, and it took next to a millisecond for him to figure out that the woman standing there was his, and likely Flash's, mate.

Flash was too stressed and caught up in the poltergeist's antics to take notice. Cassandra ... Greg had told him her name ... impressed him with her stoicism in response to Flash's clumsy, often womanizing turns of phrases, letting it bounce off of her like a tennis ball against a rubber wall.

Her hands were a perfect blend of a female's softness and a handyman's sturdy grit. He thought he spotted some calluses on her palms when shaking hands, ones that were no doubt attained through the risky climate of her choice of occupation. She had a small frame, but she was lean, strong, and likely flexible.

The thought of her letting her hair come loose from her bindings and stripping naked for him made his cock twitch in his pants, which he yanked to prevent any further awkwardness.

He led Cassandra upstairs after snarling at Flash to get his shit together and clean up the shattered vase.

"You can't talk to people like that," Slade said through gritted teeth.

Flash was hunched over, groaning like he had been hit with a boulder as opposed to a tiny glass encasement for flowers.

"Maybe I was hoping a good fuck would distract this damn thing," he grunted.

Slade left him to brood while showing

Cassandra the room where there was the most activity. It was a general study and lounging room he and Flash frequented, often on dark lonely nights when neither had a woman to bed to distract them from their various sorrows.

She walked ahead of him, posture as perfect as an arrow, black heels clicking against the hardwood floor. He imagined her in a witch's costume, a scantily clad, leather getup that elevated her breasts and plump ass as she cast away demons with her piercing piston-focused eyes.

Her scent swirled into his mouth, sending tingles to his very soul. He wanted to talk to her casually, to get to know her beyond the scope of their professional interactions.

Slade scolded himself as she placed one of her bags on the coffee table, a roaring fire behind her acting as the most appropriate backdrop to the scene.

"I need a second to get a sense of the room," she said sternly. "Do you mind?"

It took Slade a long, fat second for the penny to drop, but eventually, he nodded and held his hands up in front of him.

"Take your time," he said, voice shaking

uncharacteristically. "Let me know when you need anything."

She gave him a small, cordial smile, then began removing her things from her bag with the Navy SEAL emblem.

Slade didn't want her to have to ask again, so he hurried out of the room, using the chance to call his sister Jenny. She was a young pup who was taking full advantage of her freedom and shifter wares. They had lost both of their parents recently, and though Slade had been able to take the loss in stride, he feared his younger sister was going to use it as an opportunity to fly off the handle.

When he called, she rarely answered. He always imagined the worst of the worst, like she was lying in some ditch after hooking up with the wrong guy. He didn't often leave messages, but as he stood peering over the railing of the stairway into their dim, medieval-like hallway, his frustration got the best of him.

"You know Mom and Dad are rolling in their graves about what you're doing," he said, snarking. "You need to get your fucking shit together and grow up because they aren't here to ground you anymore."

He punched the red end-call button, nearly

cracking the screen in half. He slipped the phone into his pocket and closed his eyes for a quick moment.

It was enough dealing with what was going on with Phar-Scape, plus coping with Flash's extreme mood swings, and on top of that, he had a sister who never slept in the same place twice. It wasn't his place as her brother, but she clearly needed someone to yank on the leash every now and then.

Slade did what he could to get himself together. He felt oddly self-conscious about having Cassandra's eyes on him, which added another irritating layer to his state of mind.

But he managed to put an even, intrigued look on his face as he returned to the lounge. His stomach churned when he saw Flash sitting in a chair opposite her, slumped over with his legs spread wide like the most ignorant male on the planet.

When Flash saw him enter the room, he held out a single, open hand.

"Do you see this shit?"

Slade ignored him and glanced over to see Cassandra had removed what looked like a ventriloquist dummy from one of her larger sacks of tricks. It wore a purple velvet suit and looked like a comical display of a mafia's wardrobe.

"What the fuck is this?" Flash asked.

Cassandra had been narrowly focused on removing what looked like different shaded candles, crystals, and herbs from her bag then laid the dummy in the center of the circle. She looked up with a flicker at Slade, her lips pursing in annoyance.

"Do you want me to start with the dummy puns already?" she asked, shooting daggers in Flash's direction.

"What, are you going to play with fucking dolls until the thing decides to leave?"

Slade tried to stand in front of his friend, who was still too wound up to realize who he was talking to. Slade wanted to place a hand on her wrist and let her know that at the depths of Flash's heart and soul, he truly wasn't the vain asshole he appeared to be.

"The ritual involves summoning the poltergeist into the doll," Cassandra began, setting the doll up straight. "Once it possesses the doll, we destroy it, hence destroying the entity."

Slade watched as she spoke with an expert tone, her cadence void of wit and personality. He assumed she had met big idiots in her life, given that she was a woman. And a woman who was even remotely attractive and intelligent had their constant spats with enough utter fools to fill a Bible.

Slade nodded, placing his hands on the coffee table and leaning forward. Her blue eyes darted toward his hands like a knife slashing at his skin.

"Please don't touch the circle," she snapped.

Slade snapped his hands away, then took a step back. Her eyes were on the circle, herbs, crystals, and candles, but Slade still found it difficult to look at her. He had never been so taken with someone so quickly. That was a spell in itself.

"I'm going to light the candle and start the ritual," she said. "The beginning is likely to antagonize the spirit, so you may easily get hit in the crossfire of flying items in the room. I suggest you leave if you don't want to suffer its wrath."

She looked up at Flash briefly, a mischievous smile crossing her pink lips. The look made Slade want to taste her.

"We'll be fine," Flash snapped back. "Just get this shit done already."

"Is it better if we leave?"

He felt Flash's stare burning a hole into the

back of his head, but Slade didn't care. He was already willing to walk across fiery coals for the woman that stood before him.

She shook her head. "No difference. Just stay mindful, is all."

Slade sat on the couch opposite Flash, who gave him a glower that only the closest of friends could comprehend without words.

Cassandra proceeded to light the six candles that surrounded the dummy, breathed in deeply, then closed her eyes. The fire behind her silhouetted her frame, which merely enhanced her bountiful bosom and muscular thighs.

Slade made himself focus, listening to her chant in what he thought was maybe Latin. She held her palms open, and as soon as her voice slid up an octave, decorative plates pinned to the wall sailed across the room and crashed against the coffee table.

"Fuck!" Flash screamed.

Anything that was loose in the room came forward in a cascade of movement, swirling toward where Cassandra stood with her arms outstretched. She stood as still as a statue while the dummy on the table began to rattle against the surface, its wooden feet and hands drumming like a musician's solo.

She rolled her tongue around in words that Slade didn't understand, but the sigh of the pink appendage turned him on in ways he wouldn't ever want to admit. She had so much strength and power, and he wanted to know both of them intimately.

Eventually, the drumming of the dummy against the table ceased, along with the swirl of loose items around the room. Cassandra's eyes snapped open the moment everything in the room came to a standstill.

Slade found himself holding his breath as the dummy began to float in the air, then took one step, then another, and darted in his and Flash's direction.

They instinctively shifted into their wolf forms, with him bursting out in fiery-red fur and Flash in shades as black as night. Flash captured the dummy in his jaws, snapping it in half, while Slade took its loose legs in his mouth and ripped them like splitting a twig in half.

Slade then whipped the doll into the fireplace, where it exploded with a hail of a firestorm at the moment of impact. Cassandra remained impartial, watching them as they shifted back into human form, standing before her utterly nude.

She crossed her arms, and that devilish smirk returned. She had a way of peering under her eyelids that made her even more mysterious and, thus, alluring.

"That was certainly different," she said, voice dusky and palpable in the dim.

Flash didn't give a shit that his cock was swinging in the wind, but Slade did. He took his ripped T-shirt from the floor and covered his private bits, much to Cassandra's amusement.

She let that pink delight slip between her lips again as she began to gather up her things and place them in her pack of wonders.

"Now, if you gentlemen don't mind," she said, "I have work to get to in the morning."

Slade frantically searched his mind for something to say to keep her here while Flash tried strapping on what was left of his mangled underwear.

"Where do you work?" Slade asked politely.

As she spoke casually, she was still putting her things back in her bag, carefully and delicately, like it was all made of glass. "I work at Phar-Scape."

Slade didn't have even a millisecond to respond. He felt Flash's heart surge with rage as he lunged at Cassandra, wrapping his meat hooks of a hand around her throat. He slammed her small body against the wall next to the fireplace and snarled at her with foam pouring from his receding gum.

"What did you just say?" he growled so deeply that the items that had been cast onto the floor shook like an earthquake.

Slade stood there with his own dick swinging, eyes wide and terrified.

CHAPTER 5
CASSANDRA

Having the massive wolfman's paws around her throat felt like more of an inconvenience than a threat for Cassandra. She had felt him coming, of course, and could have diverted out of the way, leaving him space to slam into the fireplace and likely send the stone into shambles. But she thought better of it, letting him wrap his hand around her jugular and push her small frame into the wall, making the picture frames swing in fear.

It was all to save some time and money. She wasn't going to be responsible for any more damages. Plus, the man had already given her the impression of being the unhinged one, while Slade was more even and rational.

"FLASH!" Slade bellowed from the other side of the room, pressing a torn shirt over his exposed genitals. Flash hadn't taken the same precautions, letting his manhood blow free as he pressed his large body against hers. If the context were remotely different, Cassandra might have thought that it was a little bit kinky.

"FLASH, PUT HER DOWN!"

Slade slid closer laboriously, cautiously, as he approached the man drooling over exposed fangs, the hazel swirl of his eyes fading into the black pools of a doll's glare. It would have been scarier if she didn't have her handy switchblade, which she always carried on her person … she was a demon hunter, for fuck's sake … pressed against his pubic bone.

There was something about the way he held her neck; it was firm, of course, and kept her dangling a couple feet off the floor, but he hadn't applied any more pressure despite appearing furious beyond comprehension.

She jiggled the knife in her hand, scraping the tip ever so slightly over his exposed pelvis. He noticed, flicking his wide eyes down and then back up at her at lightning speed.

"So …" she began, diverting her eyes down to

where the knife spun in small circles. Her voice croaked with the slightly restricted air, but that still didn't bother her. "Do you want to talk about this with me on the floor? I explain things better on even ground."

His breath was rank with rage, and his chest rose and fell like a storm. But Cassandra managed to remain calm in the face of anger that sent most people scurrying like a mouse under a spotlight.

He seemed to realize the error of his ways, his snarl fading quickly. He lowered her to the ground, and she removed the switchblade immediately, keeping it palmed just in case.

Flash's hand around her neck lingered for a moment but soon fell, finger by finger, to the big man's side. Immediately, Slade came to them, taking Flash by the wrist like a toddler in trouble.

"Go get dressed," he hissed at him.

Flash's chin drooped to his chest, and he walked away, looking comical in his nakedness, size, and downtrodden physicality.

Cassandra smirked, then she flicked the switchblade back into its holster and slipped the device into her side pocket.

Slade came over, having clothed himself in an oversized silk robe, hands cupped in apology.

"Are you okay?" he asked, blue eyes brimming with concern.

Cassandra shrugged, then tapped the pocket where the switchblade hid.

"This isn't the first time I've been pressed up against a wall in a choke hold," she said, flashing him a sly grin.

Cassandra wasn't a woman who needed saving, but she appreciated Slade's concern nevertheless. The look of his strained expression was quickly replaced by one of embarrassment, raising both hands to his face and rubbing his eyes fervently.

"I hope you can excuse him," he said, pressing his thumbs hard into his eyeballs. "He has been through some trauma related to Phar-Scape."

Cassandra raised an eyebrow, intrigued. She moved to the table where she had laid out her things for the ritual, then stood there, posture as straight as the queen's guard, the tips of her fingers tapping lightly against the desk.

"Tell me more," she said.

Slade stopped rubbing his eyes abruptly, then looked at her, brows furrowed. His bonfire hair was still messy but sexy, to Cassandra's quick observational skills. She thought that of the two,

Slade would be the one most capable of tenderness during lovemaking. She had to blink away the thought before it ran too wild in her mind.

"Well, he escaped not too long ago ... he was only nineteen when he was captured ... by Phar-Scape," Slade began, brows still furrowed. "They, uh, experimented on him, which essentially made him violent and quick to anger."

Cassandra nodded and strummed her fingers along the desk as he spoke. She wondered why he would tell her such things, especially if she had said she worked for the company. She wondered if it was because there was an innate trust that she felt in them that perhaps was mutual.

"Did you call the police? Why are they still in business?" she asked.

Anger flashed in his eyes. "We did, and it did no good. The police said they found nothing related to what we described. They said we were lucky that Phar-Scape didn't sue us for spreading rumors."

Yeah, she would believe that. Demons are sneaky sons of bitches. But, again, what did experiments on shifters have to do with what demons wanted? She wondered if it had to do with altered emotions. "He wasn't quick to anger before all that?" Her lips turned upward into a small bow.

Slade's bewildered look disappeared, and he became the even-keeled wolf shifter she had presumed he was upon first meeting. He looked more and more handsome by the second, which made Cassandra feel a little uneasy.

"You're very intuitive, aren't you?" he asked.

Cassandra felt a shiver run down her spine, and she shook it away fast.

"One has to be aware at all times when surrounded by demons," she remarked, holding his gaze. "Potentially, anyway."

Slade brought a hand to his jaw and traced the strong outline with his fingers, making Cassandra have to hold in a gasp that crawled up her throat.

"So yeah, that's why hearing the name of that place set him off. I hope you can understand that. It was a very harrowing experience for him."

Cassandra sympathized, knowing the sinister capabilities of demons intimately. If the demon was as powerful at Phar-Scape as she guessed, it would be capable of far worse atrocities than she had ever experienced in her demon-hunting career.

She moved around the desk and placed her

hands behind her back, getting closer to Slade and his forest-like sandalwood scent. She leaned against the wood edge, subconsciously realizing that her pelvis aligned with his as she pressed her chest out.

"I don't actually work for Phar-Scape," she began, her voice low and earnest. "As a demon hunter, I have been tasked with infiltrating the organization to uncover the demonic conspiracy you speak of, the one that so deeply affected your friend."

Slade's deep-sea eyes grew wide in earnest, intrigue replacing the clear exhaustion he'd had. Which probably had lasted a lot longer than Cassandra could imagine.

"Oh?" he said, stroking his chin. "And your mission would be to kill the demon?"

His tone tickled something in the back of her neck. It was jovial and childlike, like when you first accidentally touch the hand of the boy you are crushing on.

"I would have to obtain information first," she said flatly, looking down at her bag. "My organization and I don't really know what they're up to, so I need to figure that out first, then yes, hopefully, I get to kill a demon."

A smile rose on her face. It had been so long since she had been so drawn to a man. To the point that she was ready to forgo her initial mission and forget all about what was frowned upon. It said a lot about her attraction.

Her sex pulsed when he stroked his chin, tracing the keen lines of his sculptured face. It took everything within her power to keep from letting her tongue escape from her lips and paint her plump mouth with a fresh coat of saliva.

Slade snapped his fingers, which took her out of her trance.

"I hope you are thinking what I'm thinking?" he said, smirking like an Old Spice ad.

Cassandra blinked heavily, searching her mind for wolf-shifter abilities that bordered on telepathy.

"Sorry?" The words slipped from her mouth softly.

"Well, you are tasked with getting into Phar-Scape, right?" he said, moving around the desk. "And Flash and I desperately want to make those fuckers pay for what they did to him. It seems like our goals line up quite well, don't they?"

He sat on the desk beside her as she held on to her bag for dear life. She knew what he was asking, but the way he moved had cast a fresh gust of that sandalwood scent that she found so damn appealing. It tossed her thoughts around like fruit in a blender.

"I'm not entirely sure what you mean," Cassandra said, zipping up her bag and positioning it to be lifted. "I can't just go in there guns blazing and destroy this demon. I need intel first."

She was trying not to look at Slade, but he was sitting so damn close. She slowly glanced up, the handle of her bag in hand, and watched him nod with gleeful enthusiasm.

"Oh, trust me, I know," he said. "Flash will need a good talking to, but I know that once he has his focus narrowed, nothing is going to stop him."

His eyes had brightened from their previous deep-sea state, looking almost like the baby blue of a fresh summer sky. His red hair remained wild, matching his state of inquiry.

Compared to his friend, Slade was remotely reasonable. He still attained that look of potential loss of control that Cassandra had seen in many shifters before, but his gleaming eyes said he was more mindful than his counterpart in that regard.

Even Flash appealed to Cassandra, which she would hate to admit. She had kept herself studious, diligent, and focused when it came to her work, which was why she had obtained such notoriety for success. But when it came to downtime, Cassandra was inclined toward running amuck, though she hadn't allowed herself to do such a thing in what felt like a millennium.

Flash interested her in that fashion.

She squeezed the handles of her bag and looked back, which was daring, at Slade, who towered over her even though he was resting against the desk. The words came out of her mouth fast, firing like pistons, without much thought to their consequences.

"I will have to talk to my employer," she blurted. "I am content working alone."

The excitement in his eyes faded, and he looked away but maintained his position sitting near her.

"I understand that," he said. "Flash and I come in a pair, so if you do speak to your employer, let them know about that, please."

His voice was gentle, as soft as pearls she had rolled around once in her hand. It shook her to her very core with such intensity that she had to force her legs to move out of the room. She paused, standing under the archway, still engulfed by the scent she had passed through like a waterfall.

It took her a moment to notice she was holding her breath. Cassandra knew better than anyone that it was a risk to involve more than one person with such potential for volatility. Considering it was not just one but two shifters whose very nature fell under that category, she may as well have been throwing gasoline on an open flame.

Still, the idea was thrilling.

She called to him before disembarking from the entryway.

CASSANDRA

Standing in the entryway, Cassandra decided to do something she rarely allowed herself to do ... be impulsive.

She turned to Slade and told him that they had a deal. As long as they allowed her to start things off, to obtain the proper information, and they listen to her instructions, things should go smoothly. Slade agreed, nearly leaping across the room to shake her hand.

If he had pressed any harder, the bones in her hand would surely have become dust.

"You won't regret this," he said with a sly smile on his face.

Cassandra made a point to race out of the house, making sure that she didn't run into Flash and begin a whole new game of sexy avoidance. It stifled her to the point where she once again didn't realize she was holding her breath until she let it out inside the darkness of her car. She touched her chest, feeling the warm blush of arousal surging through her like lava from an erupting volcano.

She drove home, trying to think about what she would wear the next day to Phar-Scape that would make her appear not only uninteresting but also uninterested. But the thought of both Flash and Slade with their strong hands upon her kept sneaking in, tasty images of their strong, capable bodies taking turns with their mouths between her legs, then fucking her hard and fast until she bellowed to the stars in heaven ...

"Fuck," she gasped, fingering herself through her clothing.

She showered after the ritual, which was a ritual in itself, meant to rid her of the energy of the day and to sleekly guide her into the next. Except, it didn't work, nor did the selection of the jean-shaded pencil skirt and plain crisp white blouse. Cassandra had strong muscled legs, so selecting tall heels would obviously go against her desire to fade into the background.

But she imagined one of the men she had met

seeing her in the outfit. By all the annoying stereotypical standards that women had to constantly abide by, the outfit was acceptable, maybe even bordering the line of boring. But if she straightened her hair, allowing it to fall in its full length to her shoulders, and let one little button come undone on her blouse. In that case, it could easily be transformed into something she could see piled on Flash and Slade's bedroom floor.

She bit her lip, tightening her thighs again at the supremely dirty thought. It wouldn't make sense for the mission, but hell, it had been a while since Cassandra had let herself feel sexy, intentionally anyway.

Fucking them was a nice thought, but sex with coworkers was almost an assured recipe for disaster. Since they were working together, she needed to keep her urges at bay.

But she still held the heels in her fingers, knowing for a fact that her calves would look like honey-ham-hocks in them, just as tantalizing and delicious as Sunday dinner.

She laid black, six-inch shiny heels next to her ensemble and proceeded to get very little sleep.

The next day, Cassandra was welcomed into Phar-Scape for orientation. She arrived at nine a.m. sharp with four other hired workers, three of them young men with a dream in their eyes, while the other was a woman likely her own age. She looked like someone who had intentionally wound up here to hide in the world of intelligence to save herself from the glaring eyes of men, to find there was nowhere to hide from that at all.

She had orange-red hair tied up in a bun and lingered in the back of the group along with Cassandra, who stood tall and unshakeable. The woman clutched at their orientation packages, likely questioning her choice of career path.

Cassandra did her best not to be distracted by the woman's clear timidness and focused on the mission at hand. She was someone who was always aware of the effect she had on men, no matter what she wore. Her posture was constantly impeccable, her eyes never diverted from a question, and she spoke directly and assertively.

Whether subconsciously or consciously, men were drawn to her for this. But she was quick and able to bat them away like irritating buzzards.

The day was mostly straightforward and without excitement. It reminded Cassandra of the days of yore. Before she took on the familial crest of a demon hunter, she worked in a restaurant and a clothing store. The orientations were always the same, packets full of pages to sign that no one really read, along with long and outdated welcome videos. She sat next to the red-headed woman with her leg bouncing up and down beneath the table.

Before the team was set to head off to lunch, their orientation leader gave them a tour of the grounds. They were escorted to a tower that looked positively medieval, then shown around the inside of the labs along with a long row of rooms that each looked to be carved out of Orwell's *1984* classic. Noticing a lab toward the back with a door sitting ajar, Cassandra jumped to take a chance.

It seemed like a freak occurrence, but she needed to get something out of her day. So she lingered, pretending to look around like some empty-headed commoner, then slipped into the room once her group had disappeared around the corner.

Cassandra had been trained in information extraction long enough to know that time was of the essence. The lab tech may have accidentally left the door open, maybe to go to the bathroom. She slipped a USB key out of her skirt hem and jammed it into the slot, quickly downloading any information that particular terminal had on file. She didn't have time to search through it, and she would hate to come away empty-handed.

God forbid she would actually have to start working for these people.

"Come on, come on," Cassandra said, standing hunched over the computer.

The files had nearly completed their download when the door was slammed open, and Cassandra shot up, removing the USB stick with lightning speed. She tucked it into her palm as she stood upright like a Stepford wife waiting for her next instructions.

"What are you doing in here?"

It was a young lab tech, just as she had envisioned, standing at the doorway with his tie loosened and hair set in permanent bedhead. She could have sworn she caught the gleam of his fly hanging open, but she couldn't be sure.

Cassandra slipped into innocent mode, an easy mask for any woman to wear, and held up both her hands to her chest. The USB stick was tucked steadily beneath her thumb.

"Oh my God, I am so sorry!" she proclaimed, doing her best impression of Betty Boop.

She strode to him, her heels clicking against the ground like the very hooves of Satan. As her hands lowered, she discreetly concealed the USB stick into the hemline of her skirt while expertly loosening one button of her blouse with the other. It popped open in a flurry, as dramatic as any porn the young man had probably watched alone in his bedroom. She was wearing a lacy black bra that showcased her breasts like an offering to the gods.

"I was looking for the bathroom," she said, voice still high and empty as air. "I came in here curious about the computers. They're all so bright and shiny."

She smiled at the young man, whose mouth hung open like a dumb dog waiting for its dinner. Cassandra knew she had covered her ass because he remained there, holding the door open and following her with wide, prepubescent eyes. She decided to add in one last spicy gesture for the theater and shits and giggles of it all.

She brought a finger to her plump lips, then bent over slightly, enough so that her cleavage was in full view. He looked down without hiding it, like a deer gazing at the headlights of an oncoming train.

"I hope this can be our little secret," she said in

her best sultry voice. "I don't want to lose my job over this."

She turned her lip downward like an overly sexualized Jessica Rabbit. The man nodded, gulping multiple times to find his voice.

"Of course, no problem, no problem."

She thanked him profusely, then headed back down the hallway to meet her group, making sure to swing her hips like a pendulum for added effect.

The rest of Cassandra's day remained as tedious as the morning. She tried on multiple occasions to slip into a lab, but she thought getting caught again would be too risky. No amount of cleavage or animated features would save her a second time.

When she left for the day, she was greeted by the most delicious sight, one that sent a blush all the way through her chest and loins.

Flash, wearing jeans and a tight red T-shirt, leaned against a cherry-red Porsche convertible. Beyond the amusing thought that he had matched his clothing with the car, Cassandra was speechless and found herself fingering the button of her blouse.

"And what have I done to deserve this?" she said, trying to sound nonchalant.

Flash stood and removed his Ray-Bans, revealing his dark and stormy gaze.

"I want to take you out for dinner," he grunted. "To apologize for my ... behavior yesterday."

Cassandra had slung her purse over her shoulder and held the thick orientation stack of paper pressed against her chest. She was glad he wouldn't see the way she was heaving nor the way that the buttons on her shirt wanted to burst open for him.

"To apologize?" she said, smirking.

He blew out his lips impatiently.

"Slade told me that he informed you of my ... past," he said, not meeting her gaze. "It has made me more rough-around-the-edges than usual. That kind of shit really fucked me up."

Cassandra got the inclination that the man standing in front of her wasn't used to asking out pretty ladies, nor was he practiced in the art of truly being sorry. But she sympathized with the way he couldn't look at her when he spoke about the trauma, indicating things far worse than she could imagine.

She stepped toward him, feeling the urge to touch his arm for comfort, but thought better of it.

"I understand," she said. "Well, I don't have

much to report, but I can debrief you over a good plate of dinner if that's what you want."

He was finally able to slide his eyes to hers, making Cassandra weak in the knees.

"I would love for you to *debrief* me," he nearly snarled.

Cassandra had a flash of him going at her on a bed, destroying the headboard into small splinters of wood because he had fucked her so hard. She felt the sharp movement of arousal crawling up her thighs again and was ultimately thankful that she had chosen to wear the heels that made her feel like an absolute sex goddess.

She motioned toward the car with her chin. "Let's get going then. I'm starving."

Strapped into the passenger seat, Cassandra realized she was putting herself into quite a predicament. Her attraction to both Flash and Slade was undeniable, and they had agreed to work together. Should they show her any affection at all, she was going to have difficulty resisting the feel of them between her legs and in her heart.

CHAPTER 7
CASSANDRA

Cassandra couldn't believe what she was doing but told herself to go with the flow for the moment. She wasn't a person who turned away from dates, far from it. They were a way for her to wind down and let go of all the malevolence and darkness that swirled in her mind and body. If sex was on the table, she often took it if she was in the mood, but it never lasted beyond that.

Sex was fine, but the last time she had given herself to someone, it had made her feel like a right idiot. She considered herself to be a relatively intelligent individual, so the fact that an attractive man had managed to pull the wool over her eyes bothered her.

She thought about how warm she felt despite wearing a skirt and a thin blouse that was nearly transparent. Flash had taken them to a bustling bar and grill where they chatted about her work, and she felt herself fall into a comfortable pace.

She still wanted to be careful. The fire of her attraction to the man was always on the edge of her mind.

"So you got into this work because of your family?" Flashed asked, chowing down on red-hot chicken wings.

Cassandra held a burger in her hand, nodding and covering her mouth to respond.

"It's been in my family for generations," she said, having to holler a bit over the voices and music of the bar. "So I didn't really have a choice when it came down to it."

Flash picked at his teeth, a sight that wasn't exactly meant for a calendar pose, but he attracted her all the same. He was pure animalistic impulse, and there was something about that she was envious of.

He frowned, looking like his brows were going to leave a scar on his handsome, scruffy face.

"Would you have chosen it if you had a choice?"

Cassandra finished the burger, looking beyond the hunk in front of her to feign thoughtfulness.

The truth was that she didn't really know who she was beyond being a demon hunter. In a way, she was thankful for the aristocratic family history that had gifted her the genetic set of skills that made her job so easy.

But on the other hand, she hated it sometimes, usually in the depth of night when she crawled into bed alone, aching from a day's battle.

"I think so," she finally responded, peering down at her empty plate. "I've got the skills, so I may as well use them for some good, right?"

Flash wiped his hands sloppily with the napkins at their table, then placed one forearm over the other. He leaned forward with a smirk that nearly sent her panties flying off her body.

"I hear that most demon hunters work alone," he said slyly. "You are one of the few, I reckon."

Cassandra straightened her back against the seat of the booth, her walls going up.

"You heard?" she said, raising the beer glass to her lips.

"Yes," he hissed. "So why might that be, do you think?"

She rolled her eyes dramatically, ignoring the

rapid beat of her heart that only increased the longer he stared at her.

"I work better alone," she said, trying not to mutter. "I find that working with other people often gets in the way of my abilities, my plans, or the way I operate. Not everyone is able to adjust to my ..." she trailed off, caught off guard by the sight of his hulking arms.

"Your personality?" he nearly barked.

She flicked her eyes at him, intending to snarl, but the impulse disappeared just as fast as it had come. She shifted in her seat, crossing one leg over the other.

"Yes. My personality can put some people off, I suppose."

Flash ran a hand through his messy hair, and she watched him, unabashedly hypnotized by his every movement.

"I think I can relate to that," he replied. "But most women wouldn't have so readily accepted a dinner offer after my behavior yesterday."

While eating and talking, Flash had shown a glimpse of the person she had starkly seen the day before, pushing her up against the wall with his massive hand wrapped around her throat. He snapped at the servers for getting his order wrong and had even raised his voice as a man tripped over his foot. Everyone had turned to look at the prickly beast in the corner, but after every offense, he had looked back at her with the look of a puppy dog in trouble.

He knew that it was a problem. It concerned her slightly, but it was also intriguing.

She shrugged, doing her best to remain unaffected.

"A woman needs to eat after a day of infiltration," she quipped, allowing a cunning smile to grow on one side of her face.

He smiled back at her, showing off some shiny teeth for the first time with enjoyment rather than irritation. Warmth burst in her chest, and she forced herself to look down at the beer glass that was perspiring nearly as much as she was.

"They really must have done a number on you," she said gently. "I know what demons are capable of, trust me. I think I would get just as pissed off about it as you do, if not more."

Flash's smile remained, and she felt like he wasn't used to the feeling of being even remotely understood. He had a semi-hulk personality that most people shied away from. The only person who had accepted him was Slade, but he also acted as his keeper, which was bound to have some kind of negative bounce back to it.

Cassandra drank the beer, then ordered another just as the lights in the bar dimmed, bringing light to a dance floor a few steps away from their booth. Music began blaring out of cheap speakers, causing Flash to leap up from the seat like he had just won the lottery.

"Dance with me?"

His teeth were luminous in the dark, his eyes like jewels out of a black ocean. Normally, Cassandra did her best to maintain her cool, calm, and collected demeanor, which meant dancing was completely out of the question. But looking at Flash holding out his hand to her, the way the veins in his arms popped out like pipes, and the movement of carnal attraction swirling like a tornado in her belly, there was no way she was saying no.

She grinned at him and placed her hand in his palm. He pulled her up sharply, and she gasped like some kind of damsel in a drive-in flick.

"Try to keep up," he said with a wink.

They moved onto the wooden floor with his hand clutching hers, not too hard, but assertive enough. Her breasts had lightly traced over his chest when he pulled her up, so her nipples were hardening under the lace of her bra. When they hit the dance floor, she was surprised to find how confident he was, letting his hand rest upon her hips and grinding up behind her as she mimicked his relaxed state.

Cassandra felt like she was having a strange acid trip or a dream because she hadn't ever felt this comfortable with a man. But she was also aroused to the point that her insides were burning with desire for a wolf shifter she had only met the day before.

When it came to the slow dance, it was all over. She leaned against his chest while he put one hand on her hip and the other boldly slid to cup one of her ass cheeks. She lifted her head, prepared to be angry, but was instead beyond impressed.

Cassandra stared up at him with sultry eyes, needing him so badly that she thought she was going to lose her mind right then and there on the dance floor.

He looked at her, hunger as blatant as his hard-on under his jeans.

She used one hand to unbutton her blouse enough so only he could see her sexy, lacy bra. His eyes nearly burst out of their sockets.

"I want you now," she demanded with a hiss. "You need to fuck me right now, Flash."

Flash growled before pushing his lips onto hers, nearly head-butting her as she gasped and moaned with a fervor she thought she had lost to the depths of memory. She lifted her hands to tangle into his hair as the world faded away, craving him like a shark craved its prey.

His tongue wandered inside her mouth, and she felt a wet snap as he pulled away from her. He'd had her bottom lip between his teeth, sucking it, before grabbing her wrist and pulling her out of the neon lights of the dance floor and into the concealment of the dark.

Cassandra's heart pumped with exhilaration as he found a supply closet near the bathrooms. He pushed her in playfully and closed the door behind him. He grunted as he pulled her face to his, and they made out with a reckless abandon that Cassandra had yearned for, for such a long time.

He unbuckled his jeans, and she turned around. When he saw she had bent over against the wall, hiked up her skirt, and whipped down her panties for him, he released another grunt of utter approval.

"Fuck me, baby," Cassandra demanded. "Fuck me, right here, right now. I need you."

She felt desperate, but she didn't want him to notice. He popped his cock out of his pants and immediately slid himself into her wetness, causing her to let out a loud groan as she felt him fill her all the way.

"Oh fuck, Flash!" she called out.

He bucked into her hard, just the way she had imagined him doing, grabbing hold of her hips and going to town. Cassandra couldn't control herself, hammering wildly back into his thrusts and calling out as he slammed directly into her G-spot, sending shockwaves of pleasure through her body like lightning.

"Yes! Fuck, yes," she moaned.

His hands crawled from her hips up her blouse, briefly cupping her breasts under her shirt, then moved up to her neck and mouth. She once again felt his strength on her throat, but this time, he had no intention of causing her any harm.

"Shh, my bad girl," he growled into her ear, causing her skin to break out in gooseflesh. "You don't want anyone to hear us and spoil our fun, do we?"

She grinned like a madwoman as he continued

to plow into her, harder and faster, just the way she wanted, their bodies clapping into each other like riveting applause. He took the hand that had still been resting on her breast and wrapped it around her mouth, muffling her approaching cries of ecstasy.

Cassandra closed her eyes as she experienced one of the most wonderful orgasms she had ever felt in her life. It jetted from her pussy to the tips of her fingers that dug into the concrete wall in front of her. She was glad he had covered her mouth because if he hadn't, her bellows would have been heard by every single patron.

She felt high as a kite as she felt him continue to thrust inside her, so content with her naughtiness and awareness that she had broken one of her top rules.

CHAPTER 8
FLASH

Flash had never had such spontaneous and exhilarating sex in his entire life. Sure, he had been with women, but there wasn't anyone who made him feel the way Cassandra had. Her forwardness and demands for him to fuck her turned him on like a lantern in the dead of night, which made him realize that had been exactly what he was.

He felt it in his body when she came, rubbing against his cock to absorb all of the delight the dopamine surge had to offer. That was enough to force his body to follow. He exploded inside her with a thrilling orgasm, making his legs shake like twigs in the wind. He leaned against her, engulfed in the thick fog of her wonderful lemon and vanilla scent and her melodious whimpers.

It was only after they had gotten themselves together and left the storage room that Cassandra suddenly turned cold.

They were walking through the crowd to the exit, and Flash had tried to reach out his hand to grip hers. He was still floating from the fast fuck, his brain on fire from the wash of endorphins moving up and down his spine. So when she actively moved her hand away from his, the tinge of disappointment he felt in his heart was sharp.

"Are you okay?" he asked her as they wandered into the parking lot. Her heels were clapping against the ground ahead of them like a teacher late for a lesson.

The fantasy bloomed in his mind, and he stashed it away for later.

"I'm fine," she snapped at him.

His cock had barely deflated in his pants as they climbed into the car in silence. He wanted to place his hand on her thigh, that delicious muscle he'd caught mere glimpses of as they sat opposite each other in the booth. But he thought better of it, given her current state, seeing it as too bold at the moment.

So they drove on in silence, Flash's irritation rising in him like an oncoming avalanche. He was good at noticing it, but it was when it decided to fire on full force that he found himself losing control. He was thankful he had just had an orgasm that seemed to have a sedative effect on his emotions.

If he hadn't, God forbid, he'd likely have said something to her to put her off him completely.

He turned on the radio to get rid of the awkwardness and maybe even to distract himself. He commented on a few songs and ads, but all she did was nod or give him a pathetic, trivial smile. He wondered if she regretted how hard she had come onto him at the bar or if she was embarrassed that they had fucked in a storage closet.

It didn't matter because they weren't going to get anywhere that night. So when they arrived at Slade and his house, what had transpired between them was so obvious, it was nearly palpable.

Slade waited at the door with a book in his hand, about to walk into the kitchen to make himself a cup of coffee. He greeted them both politely.

"Busy night at the pub?" he asked.

"Very," Cassandra replied in a snap. "I've got

some calls to make to update my employer, so I'll be in the lounge before we talk about my day."

Without saying another word, Cassandra moved up the steps like she had been to their home a thousand times. She shut the door like a bereft teenager, and Slade held out his hands in a shrug.

"You really couldn't wait to get to her, could you?"

He and Slade had discussed the night before how Slade knew immediately that Cassandra was their fated mate. Because of their past fighting over a woman, they'd decided to come to an agreement after informing her of the whole mate thing. Except, Flash hadn't told her about the mate thing, and they'd had sex without telling her about how serious the act would be between them

"She came onto me, man," Flash whispered through gritted teeth. "You know exactly how it is. There is no way you could have said no either."

He huffed past Slade and moved into the kitchen, turning on the coffee machine and grinding the beans. He had been living with Slade for a long time, so he knew his nightly routine. They were like an old married couple. Slade walked into the kitchen, placed his book down, and leaned against the counter.

"So, did you tell her?" he asked, keeping his voice down.

"No, for fuck's sake," Flash snapped, nearly slamming the coffee beans into the grinder. "It just didn't come up, okay?"

Slade sighed and rubbed his hands over his face, a gesture Flash had grown used to. Like an exhausted father giving his son shit for being so late past curfew.

"But you decided to have sex with her anyway?" Slade pressed on.

Flash poured water into the coffeemaker and flicked the light on to green. He then leaned against the counter, his eyes bulging at his friend, nearly breaking the marble countertop beneath his grip.

"What did I just say?" Flash snarled.

"You said she came on to you."

"Yes."

"So you're the wolf shifter, am I correct?" Slade gave him a condescending look. "You are the one who knows better than her. Even if she was climbing on top of you in the middle of the bar, you were the one who had to resist her and tell her what she means to us."

Flash had the urge to leap on top of his friend and pummel him for good measure. But he wondered, even beneath the cloud of his anger, if the motivation behind the lecture was simply male jealousy. If they were both indeed her mate, then Slade would be longing for her the same way Flash was. The feeling was a near ache, and it was almost impossible to resist the temptation of sex when a mate offered.

He turned to the coffee machine, trying to let it go for the time being.

"Okay, I shouldn't have fucked her. Is that what you want to hear?" he growled. "I'm an idiot, nothing new."

He heard Slade groan next to him. Then he left the room without saying another word, hearing his footsteps as he moved up to the lounge where Cassandra was making her phone calls.

Flash made three cups of coffee, leaving one black and sugarless because he didn't know how Cassandra took it. He came into the room to find Cassandra with her ear pressed against a phone, her computer on her lap, and Slade sitting opposite her, quietly rolling his fingers in his palms.

Flash placed the mugs down, then caught a look from Cassandra, who smiled at him. Her lips still managed to glisten a bit with the lipstick she had been wearing before their dalliance in the closet, despite Flash thinking that it had been smeared. He gave her a nod, then touched his own lips instinctively, remembering her flavor vividly.

A part of him hoped the gesture got to Slade, deep in his envious bones. Though he wasn't consciously trying to head down that road again, it sure was satisfying.

He sat next to Slade in silence while Cassandra finished her phone call. She had buttoned up her shirt nearly to the top, but the bottom was pulled out from her skirt, and the skirt itself had been rolled up enough to show off a delectable patch of skin near her lovely bottom.

Flash sighed to himself, replaying their passionate romp in his mind over and over.

"Okay, sorry, guys," she said, placing the phone down.

Flash perked up, getting lost in the icy-blue glare of her eyes.

"I've sent files that I was able to obtain today to my lab assistant Greg, but the scientific language is beyond both of us. Apparently, we need to find a chemist to interpret the findings."

Slade leaned on his fist against the arm of the couch and spoke like they were sitting in a library. "I know a guy that could probably help with that," he replied.

Cassandra nodded, a brief smile passing over her lips. Flash was finding it difficult to focus on the mission ... what they had paired up to do in the first place. His cock still twitched in his pants from his attraction to the woman who he felt he could go multiple rounds with before finally tapping out due to hunger or thirst, whichever came first.

He would gladly give her some screaming orgasms that would make her forget any terrible thing that had ever happened to her.

As if to read his mind, she looked at him, brows raised in expectation.

"Do you know anyone, Flash?"

For a moment, he had forgotten what they were talking about. He sensed Slade's disapproval energy as radiant as the moon shining outside.

"Um," he stumbled, having to look away from the most gorgeous woman he had ever met. "Not that I can recall. Try Slade's contact. He knows a guy for everything."

She smiled at him again, and he thought he was going to come undone.

"It's settled then," she said, looking at the computer. "Time is of the essence, of course."

Slade nodded, then leaned forward to look at the black cup of coffee sitting in front of them.

"How do you take your coffee, Cassandra?"

She looked up at Slade, eyes glassy with exhaustion.

"A drop of cream and one sugar, if you don't mind," she said. "And call me Cass."

"It's no problem," Slade said.

He picked up the mug, then pushed past Flash's legs with intentional aggression. Flash grunted, then found Cassandra ... Cass ... peering at him like lasers cutting through the snow.

"Did you tell him?" she asked.

Flash had opened his mouth without a clue about what he was going to say. It was then he noticed a beam of light cast itself over Cass's frame, then began flicking on and off like an electric light trap for mosquitoes. There wasn't a road close to them other than the one that went the opposite way, and the lounge was on the other side of the house entirely.

"What's wrong?" Cass asked.

Flash rose from the couch, stepping to the window behind her. It was only a few feet from her, so he caught her scent again, that lemon and captivating vanilla. It would have been enough to send his lips to hers again. Sneaking in a little tongue before Slade got back with the coffee would have been sexy and daring.

If it wasn't for that light that caught his eye and made his heart beat in his chest rapidly beyond his attraction to the enchanting demon hunter sitting before him, he would have. Instead, he pushed at the thin drapes and narrowed his wolf focus at the window, searching through the trees for activity.

Lo and behold, almost a mile away, sat a car with its lights on. The lights flashed, washing everything around the car in tones of yellow and orange. The average human would have cast it aside as fireflies, maybe even a light catching from a distant road. But Flash had impeccable vision, and what he had initially feared had come to fruition.

"What is going on, Flash?" Cass said, sounding more worried.

"Someone followed us."

CHAPTER 9

SLADE

After Flash informed him about their visitor, Slade glared out the window, using his keen eyesight to focus on the van. He was sure the occupants of the vehicle didn't know they were being watched. Even though he wanted a better look, he held back from moving the curtain.

He was worried that Flash might do something impulsive ... *when didn't he* ... but to Slade's surprise, Flash didn't make any sudden moves. He'd half expected his friend to throw the curtains aside and point at the van, screaming, *I see you!*

"Can't see much," Flash said, tilting his head to see through the edge of the glass frame.

"I know," Slade muttered, frustrated. He and

Flash were far enough back from the glass that even if those in the van were shifters, they most likely didn't know they were being observed.

If they weren't shifters, then they didn't have to be careful at all. Humans would be easy to stalk, and in Slade's opinion, trying to sneak up on shifters this way would make the humans look like they had suicidal tendencies.

"I don't want to just sit here and wait for them to attack," Flash muttered. Slade's anxiety rose a notch as he anticipated having to restrain his friend. It didn't matter if there was a ten-foot tentacled monster in the van. Flash would go after it as if he were invincible.

Cass moved across the room so she could peek through the gap in the curtains without being seen. Slade admired her calm, smooth movements. She was completely self-assured and confident, like the best fighters always were. She barely disturbed the air as she walked like a ninja that could appear and disappear at will.

He couldn't help admiring her other attributes too. Her slow movements made him notice her long, sleek thighs, supple waist, and firm breasts. For a few seconds, he forgot they were in potential danger and watched the low light in the room cascade over her golden hair.

"Hey, bro," Flash snapped. "You with us?"

"Yes, of course, sorry," Slade said. Obviously, Flash had been speaking for some time, and Slade had been completely out of it.

How can I help myself? Look at her.

"The lady was talking," Flash muttered, disgusted. Slade shook his head, amused. Cass turned, and he could see her eyes gleaming with a hint of mischief.

"I said that the van is probably tailing me," Cass said.

What a nice tail it is too.

"It could be to do with the demon hunting. I definitely piss off a lot of groups with that. Or it might be because of my hack job at Phar-Scape. Who knows?"

"But you don't think it's here for us?" Slade asked. She shook her head.

"Have you guys ever had any issues being followed before you brought me home?"

"No," Flash said, looking out the window again. "No one would fucking dare."

"So, there's a good chance these guys don't

even know who you are, and they just want me," Cass said, stepping back from the window.

Who doesn't?

"I've got a plan," Flash said, grinning. Slade cringed, waiting to hear his best friend's solution. He was pretty sure it was going to involve an unbelievable amount of violence and risk. Flash was also difficult to talk out of something once he had a course of action stuck in his head.

"I'll go through the garage and find that novelty blow-up doll and take her for a ride in the Porsche," Flash said. "If they're after Cass, the van should follow me."

"You think I can be that easily mistaken for a blow-up doll?" Cass asked dryly. Flash laughed.

"It's got a nice blonde wig. If I wrap a coat around it and prop it up on the front seat, I don't think anyone will be able to tell the difference."

"I'm positively insulted," Cass muttered, her grin showing she was more amused than insulted.

"I like the plan," Slade said, relieved that Flash's idea didn't involve bolting across the lawn and hurling Molotov cocktails at the unknown vehicle.

"Thanks," Flash said, laughing. "You don't always support my plans."

"This one is decent," Slade answered.

"I can keep them busy for hours if need be," Flash said. "If they don't like following me around, I'll park in an alley and jump around to steam up the windows."

"Flash," Slade muttered, putting a hand over his face. Flash just laughed, and to Slade's surprise, Cass did too.

"If it doesn't follow, then we have our answer," Cass said, peeking through the curtains again. "You can circle back, and we'll coordinate to take these guys out properly."

"If it does chase Flash, then we can slip out in one of the other cars," Slade said. "We'll head upstate to my friend, the chemistry whiz, and get these pages analyzed."

"Let's get on it," Flash said. "I don't want to give these guys any time to plan anything or make a move on us."

Slade watched Flash head out the door, and he and Cass waited, watching the van. After a few minutes, Flash took off through the garage doors and headed for the main road. A few seconds after the Porsche had passed, the van followed it.

"That answers that question," Cass whispered. "It is me they want."

"Does it bother you?" Slade asked. Cass shook her head.

"Not really. I mean, it does, but we've got more important things to take care of right now. Obviously, I want to know who it is and why they want me. They'll show their intentions sooner or later, though. Will Flash be okay by himself?"

"Are you kidding me?" Slade laughed. "He'll have a great time. The biggest worry here is that he gets bored, pulls them into a fight, and tears them to shreds before we find out what they want."

Cass laughed softly. "Always such a rage machine."

Slade lost his smile immediately, shaking his head slowly.

"Not always. But let's not dwell on that right now. We have things to do."

Cass agreed, and they headed to the garage to get into Slade's Cadillac SUV. As they pulled out onto the road, Slade noticed that Cass was tense, sitting as far away from him as she could with her arms folded. He was excited to spend a bit of time alone with her, and he wondered if she was nervous about being with him.

The situation with Flash. That's got to be it.

"You don't need to worry," Slade said, trying to put her at ease. "Flash isn't the jealous type, and neither am I."

He glanced over and saw her big, blue eyes focused on him. She looked curious but still guarded.

"In fact, I think you might be fated to be with us ... both of us. You could be our mate."

Cass laughed, a sudden, loud noise that cracked the silence apart.

"Then your fate sucks," she said, shaking her head. "I'm not the most pleasant person to be around, and my life is extremely dangerous."

Slade laughed. "So is ours. We like danger, honey. Don't worry about that for even a second."

He glanced at her staring at him. When their eyes met, Slade felt a bolt of connection between them that was more powerful than anything he'd ever felt.

I'd face any kind of danger just to be with you.

"I find you very pleasant to be around," he said softly.

Talk about an understatement. Sitting next to you is more thrilling than base jumping.

Cass actually blushed a little.

"Thank you ... I don't hear things like that

very often," she said. He saw her face twist into a scowl as she turned away to look out the window.

"In fact, I've heard some pretty terrible things about what it's like to be in my company, and none of it described me as pleasant."

"I'd say that person's opinion doesn't count," Slade said firmly. "Like, seriously. Fuck them. Why would you care about something negative someone told you?"

"Because we always believe the ones we love the most, even if what they call 'love' isn't love at all."

Her voice was so soft, almost beyond his wolf ears. He sensed great pain in her tone and wondered if she was referring to a lost love that must have hurt her terribly.

An unreasonable wave of rage crested through him. If he found out that another male had hurt her, he might have to hunt the beast down and tear him limb from limb.

I will never let her be hurt like that, ever again.

He changed the subject tactfully, telling her a little about his life in the pack and how his main motivation was to protect his sister. The miles passed swiftly, and by the time they arrived at his friend's house, both of them were relaxed and enjoying each other's company.

Slade parked the SUV in Schindler's driveway, then led Cass around the side to a back door. The manor was huge, and the front doors were always locked. At a side entrance, Slade gave a light knock.

"Will he be awake?" Cass asked, checking the time.

"Yes," Slade said. "I don't think he ever sleeps. He has a few servants who are always around, anyway."

The door gave an impressively spooky squeak as it slowly swung open. Slade greeted the small man who opened it, asking for Schindler. They were directed down the hall to the study.

"What was that?" Cass muttered. "My demon sense went a bit haywire when he looked at me."

"Magical shifter," Slade answered. "Probably doing some late-night conjuring. I think he's naturally a mouse shifter but plays with all kinds of magic. He's very useful at keeping an eye on the house and grounds."

"I can imagine," Cass said. "I hope I don't have to kick his ass sometime."

Slade grinned, thinking that a mouse shifter

with a few nasty spells wouldn't have much chance against her. He guided her to the study where his elderly friend was bent over a chemistry set, focused intently on a bubbling beaker.

"Slade," Schindler cried without looking up. "Did you know there are shifters on earth that don't conform to natural DNA patterns? I have no idea where these guys came from. Every time I analyze their blood, it gets too volatile."

As if to prove his point, the beaker exploded. Schindler grabbed a fire extinguisher and blasted the bubbling green goo, trying to escape across the table.

"Insane," he muttered. When Schindler finally looked up, he did a double take.

"Oh, my. You've brought a lady," Schindler said. He hurried over to shake Cass's hand.

"Nice to meet you," she said, smiling.

"And you," Schindler said. "I'm assuming you have something for me, and this isn't a social visit."

"No," Slade agreed, gesturing for Cass to get her printout. She handed it to Schindler, who gazed intently at the pages.

"My, my," he muttered, sitting down and flipping through the codes. "This will take me some time. Let Mickey show you to a room to rest, would you? This could take a while."

Schindler waved a hand dismissively, and Slade and Cass backed away. The mouse shifter appeared behind them, giving Cass a bit of a start. Neither of them had heard him approach.

Mickey escorted them to a room, and Slade was excited to see it only had one huge bed. Cass looked at him, one eyebrow raised in query. "So, you want to share, or shall I take the floor?"

"It's a big bed," Slade said, sitting and patting it encouragingly. To his excitement, Cass took the hint and sat next to him.

He turned toward her, ready to make small talk to soften the moment. To his surprise, she leaned forward and kissed him, her hot, wet lips instantly finding his. A bolt of pure, flaming pleasure shot through him, setting his skin on fire and muddling his mind. Only one thought was completely clear.

She is our mate!

CASSANDRA

Cassandra simply couldn't stop herself from kissing Slade the second she sat next to him on the bed. She had been drawn to him from the first moment she laid eyes on him and the casual intimacy they'd shared on the way to Schindler's house only enhanced her desire.

His talk about them being mates had unsettled her because she didn't know if she wanted to become fully entangled with these guys ... either of them ... let alone both at the same time. The heat in her body wouldn't be denied, though. She couldn't sidle up so close to this hunk of male gorgeousness without making a move.

Slade kissed her back, and she leaned into him,

her hands coming up to stroke his shoulders as she pulled him to her. Even though he was reciprocating, he wasn't hurling her onto the mattress with unerring vigor the way she'd expected.

Cass pulled back, trying to catch her breath as she looked into his eyes. Desire burned in his gaze, as well as something darker and more intense that he seemed to be struggling against.

"Are you okay?" she whispered, holding herself back with extreme effort. She had broken the kiss, but she still held onto his shoulders. Her fingertips traced little circles against his shirt as she imagined the soft, warm skin underneath the fabric.

"Yes," he whispered, his breath hot against her lips. "I didn't want to presume ... since there is only one bed. I mean ..."

Cass chuckled, sliding even closer to him. "Clearly, I'm the one making the first move," she said, kissing him lightly. "So, you can keep your gentlemanly status if that's what you're worried about."

She kissed him again, making sure any protest from him was obliterated by her passion. Cass explored his lips and tongue with her own for a few moments, enjoying the fire that built inside her and slowly emanated through her core, flooding her limbs with anticipation.

He reached out and held her waist gently, not putting any pressure on her. Cass let her hands roam down his arms, feeling the hard muscles. When he flexed under her hands, she moaned and tightened her grip on him, wriggling forward to slip onto his lap.

She pulled back, looking into his eyes as she gently stroked his cheek. The throbbing inside rushed through her, an intense need that wiped out rational thought. His eyes focused on her face, and she could tell he was struggling for control.

Lose control. Go further than you ever have. Just let go!

To her frustration, he stayed completely still, as if he was determined to let her take the lead. Cass reached down and grabbed the tail of her shirt, ripping it over her head and throwing it aside.

Slade gasped, and she didn't pause as she reached behind to unfasten her bra. Cass pulled it off and hurled it away, looking down to see Slade's reaction.

His eyes were fixed on her breasts. She tightened her thighs against his, stretching up and leaning back to put her nipples right next to his mouth. She heard him groan as his arms went around her waist, and his lips found her skin.

Cass sighed in pleasure as Slade's hands roamed up her back, and his mouth moved across her breasts. He teased her nipples with the tip of his tongue and sucked on them with slick, hot lips. The arousal shot through her, awakening deep within her.

She ground against him, thrusting her hips back and forth as he devoured her breasts. When he slid his hands down and grabbed her ass, she shrieked in surprise, sitting up and leaning forward to wrap her hands around the back of his head.

She pressed his face into her chest, smothering him. He moaned and pulled her more tightly against him as if he wanted to drown there, lost between her firm breasts.

Cass writhed up and down, the throbbing in her core so intense, it was almost painful. She pushed Slade back and tugged on his shirt from the shoulders, hearing a small, frustrated cry coming from her own throat. Slade grinned as he pulled off the shirt, but Cass only got a glimpse of the smile before her eyes were captured by his incredible, hard body.

She ran her fingers across his chest and abs, eyes wide with wonder. Her fingertips felt as if they'd become super sensitive, letting her map every inch of his skin and the rock-hard muscles beneath.

Her gaze ran down his body until she came to the belt of his pants. She frowned, letting out a sharp noise of frustration. Cass held his shoulder with one hand and pointed at the belt, sending her fury into the magic in her hands. The belt undid itself and slid free of the loops all by itself to fly across the room, where it hit the wall with a violent thump.

"Ah, Cass ..."

"Shh!" she snapped, not looking up. She put both hands on his shoulders and slammed him back against the bed, then pushed off the mattress to flip her legs out so that her feet landed neatly on the floor.

Almost as part of the same movement, she grabbed the waistband of his pants and gave a sharp tug. Slade lifted his hips obligingly, and Cass practically tore the pants off his legs. She went to get on top of him and realized she still had her own pants on.

Before she could undo them, Slade's hands covered hers. She watched him slowly undo the button and zipper, then roll the pants gently down her legs until they fell at her ankles.

Her breathing came faster and faster. Slade stared at her underwear as if he could see through it. Arousal raged through her, crashing through her blood and making her throb deep inside. She was almost trembling with need but felt trapped by Slade's careful attention.

He reached out, brushing his fingers against the waistband of her panties. Cass gasped, shivering with anticipation. Slade's strong fingers grabbed the flimsy fabric and, with a hard tug, ripped them down her legs.

Cass's desire increased tenfold, her blood running so hot that she moaned and bent her hips toward him. Slade wrapped one arm around her waist to pull her close and pressed his lips to her pussy, his hot, wet tongue sliding through her aching lips to find her clit.

Cass grabbed his head, leaning back and opening her thighs to invite him deeper. Slade's hands tightened on her hips, sliding around to grab her ass. She let her body go limp as he stroked her with his tongue, teasing at going lower while he lapped at her clit, sucking on it.

Slade increased his pace, and Cass grabbed his head even harder, thrusting her hips up and down. As she came, a series of moans ripped from her throat, the orgasm flooding through her with so much force she couldn't hold herself up.

She sagged into Slade's arms, and he stood, lifting her and turning to throw her onto the bed. Cass's limbs were loose. Her whole body relaxed as she fell, spread-eagled on the mattress. His hands on her thighs opened her legs wide, his touch moving along her hips as he plunged his mouth into her pussy again.

She shrieked, thrashing under him. Slade teased at her deeper folds, his tongue probing into her and making her come again. When he stopped, she was shivering and senseless with one hand over her face as she shook her head back and forth.

The bed moved as he climbed up on top of her, and Cass took a few deep breaths. When nothing happened, she looked up to find Slade's face hovering over her own.

He held her gaze as he thrust his hips toward

her. The hard, hot head of his cock pressed against her wet pussy, and she moaned, twisting her body closer to his.

"Yes?" he asked. She nodded, reaching up to grab his shoulders so she could touch him.

"Fuck, yes," she cried. "Fuck me."

Slade gripped her shoulder with one hand as he reached down with the other. He teased her with one finger before grabbing his cock and pressing it against her folds. He moved very slowly, and Cass reached down, grabbing his ass as she growled in frustration.

"Fuck me, now," she cried, digging her fingernails into his ass cheeks as she thrashed under him. His hard cock slid into her, and she moaned as she took him in, shoving her hips up and down until they were completely locked together.

For a moment, she held tightly to him, looking up at the ceiling as she focused on the inner workings of her body. Cass let her hands trail up his back until she could link her fingers under his shoulder blades, opening her thighs to cross her ankles under his ass. Slade groaned, his breath hot against the side of her face.

She turned her mouth to his, and their lips met. As their tongues tangled, she squirmed against him, crying out when his hard cock moved deep inside her. As the kiss intensified, Slade braced his hands against the mattress and began to thrust in long, slow movements.

Cass held on to him with her knees and hands, kissing him as hard as she could. His strokes became harder and faster as if their bodies had fallen into perfect time. She was throbbing with multiple extended orgasms, so lost in pleasure that all she could feel was the raging hot desire flooding every fiber of her being.

Slade let out a long, harsh gasp. He reared back, watching her as his hips took on an even more urgent rhythm. Cass stared into his beautiful eyes, watching the pleasure and desire darken his gaze as he was flooded with primal need. She felt him thicken inside her, and the passion was too much.

She threw her head back and screamed, clinging to him. Slade's breath came in a hard, steady rush as he thrust into her with complete abandon. Just as her deepest muscles wrapped around him and spasmed into a massive, earth-shattering orgasm, Cass heard his own cry as his cock throbbed and spurted deep inside her.

Cass panted, holding on to Slade with every

inch of her body. His heart pounded against hers. She could tell by the throbbing of his body that he wasn't done yet, and his stamina and desire excited her even more.

Who needs sleep when you could be a mess of pleasure, caught in the hands of a man like this?

Cass wriggled in his arms, turning her face to find his lips again. They kissed slowly, deeply, their bodies so enmeshed that she felt him getting hard for her again. She wrapped her legs around him and thrust toward him eagerly as her own body awakened to a lust she'd never known.

CHAPTER 11
FLASH

When the van followed him, Flash felt a surge of triumph as well as excitement. He was looking forward to screwing over these guys, whoever they were.

As he took a side street that would lead him through quieter areas, he toyed with ideas about how to deal with them. It might be a good plan to find out who they were and what they wanted, but finesse wasn't Flash's strong point.

The anger rose inside him like a red wave. Knowing they were after his mate was feeding an intense fury that was almost blinding. He was tempted to pull over to the side of the road right then and there and take them all on.

I have to give Slade time to get away. If I want to take these guys on, I need to get as far from Cass as possible before I do.

He had no doubt that once the guys in the van realized Cass was not with him, they would turn around. Flash had to make sure that didn't happen. Eliminating the threat to his mate was far more important than finding out who these guys were.

Flash glanced into the rearview mirror. The driver hung back, doing a very poor job of pretending not to follow. Flash took a few narrow side streets, daring the van to keep up with him.

As he rounded a corner to a bigger road, he didn't see the van pull in behind him. For a brief, anxious moment, he thought he'd lost them.

That's just great. I lost the tail when I was supposed to be letting him chase me. Now I'll have to go back and find him.

Flash slowed, letting the Porsche coast down the street. He was wondering how to go about chasing down the bad guys when the van suddenly pulled out in front of him.

"I'm impressed," he muttered. With a huge grin, he slammed his foot down on the gas pedal and sped toward the van. A few guys had gotten out already, fanning across the road. They leapt out of the way as Flash put the car into high gear and drove straight at them.

At the last second, he ripped the wheel to the side. The Porsche turned violently, sliding sideways toward the van with an ear-splitting squeal of ruined rubber against the asphalt. He had timed it perfectly, and even though his car tapped the side of the van, there was little damage.

Instantly, five guys jumped onto the Porsche. There was a massive thump on the roof as one landed there, and the Porsche rocked as two guys jumped onto the trunk and another on the hood. The last one leered through the passenger window, glaring at Flash.

The guy looked at the blow-up doll briefly, a flash of anger showing in his eyes.

"You took us on quite a ride, you know that?" he said. Flash grinned.

"Not over yet, asshole," Flash yelled. He threw the car into gear and gunned it. The Porsche screamed in protest but took off in a massive cloud of smoke, making all the guys tumble off onto the road.

Flash was tempted to turn around and just mow them all down, but he wanted to get his hands dirty. After the thrill of the chase, he was aching for a decent, challenging fight. He hoped these guys were up to the task. It would leave him very disappointed if he slaughtered them in only a few minutes.

He leapt out of the Porsche and shifted on his first stride, becoming the wolf as he ran. Fury rose in his chest, and he let it loose as a long, drawn-out howl. The five men were just picking themselves up from the road. Flash jumped at the nearest one and tore out his throat.

As he twisted to go for the next man, something landed on top of him. It was massive, heavy, and had claws that were as strong as a steel vise with razors on its edges.

After jumping and twisting and only getting his back torn up for the effort, he eventually threw himself to the ground and rolled, dislodging the thing. As he jumped up, he saw it was a big, ugly vulture.

Flash darted in to kill it when he was hit by a massive punch. He turned and squared up, facing a bear shifter. The other two guys were still in human shape, and Flash didn't know if they were shifters or not. One of them had an ax, the other a wicked-looking chain.

The vulture was getting up, and so was the bear. Flash focused on the bear and lowered himself, ready to spring.

The bear rose onto its hind legs and roared. Flash charged, curving to the side as if he were going for the vulture. When the bird lifted and the bear lunged at him, Flash ducked under its claws and latched on to the fur-covered neck.

The bear roared, staggering away and swiping at him with his claws. Flash hung on, sinking his teeth deep into the bear's throat before shaking and twisting his head. The bear tried to run, but Flash tightened his hold until the bear went down.

He barely had time to release his jaw before he felt the sting of the chain on his hind legs. He was jerked onto the road, and the breath slammed out of him. He struggled briefly, but the chain was too tight. Flash relaxed, sagging against the pressure as if he was knocked out.

"Is he down?" one of them yelled.

"I don't know. He looks out to me."

"He killed Barry!"

"What, you didn't realize this job was dangerous when you filled out the application?"

Flash held in a chuckle. He hated to kill a guy

with a good sense of humor. It was just a pity they were on opposite sides.

The two guys crept closer while the vulture waited on top of the van. When they stopped right by his head, Flash heard one of them pull out a gun.

"This was too easy," the guy said.

Flash sprang up from the ground. He threw himself at the nearest guy and tore out his neck. They had been standing so close together that the other man was knocked over too. The tension had gone out of the chain, and Flash was able to get free of it as he crawled over the dead guy to rip open the other one.

Above him, the vulture screamed. Flash turned toward it, growling. He was ready to send it to the birdie afterlife when he suddenly heard the rumble of approaching engines.

"Fuck!" he muttered, glancing around the side of the van. Several cars were approaching at high speed. The vulture cackled in glee.

Flash turned and ran back to the Porsche, shifting as he escaped. He gunned the engine, tearing away down the street. The cars followed him, swerving dangerously across the road. Flash pulled away from them, managing to lose a few cars as he twisted through the streets, finally losing the last one near the turnpike.

Once he was sure he'd lost them, he turned for home. He was grinning by the time he got there, imagining Slade and Cass all tied up in sweaty knots together. He hoped Slade had made his move and that he'd know Cass was the one.

We are all meant to be together.

When he got there, the house was dark. Flash waited for a second, debating what to do. He could stay here and wait around or follow them to Schindler's. Flash decided to head to Greg's to try to make progress on the Phar-Scape situation. He wondered humorously if he owed Greg a present for bringing him, Slade, and Cass together.

He had absolutely no doubt that Cass would be back on the job as soon as possible, and he didn't want her going in alone. Greg could hack in and get him access to the company, so he could cover Cass's ass while she did her undercover thing.

When he arrived, he banged on the door until Greg opened it. His friend was rubbing sleep from his eyes and yawning as he pulled open the locks.

"What the fuck, man? It's like, three a.m.," Greg muttered.

"Yeah, well. I've got a job for you, and I want it done before dawn."

"What did I do to deserve a friend like you," Greg muttered.

"Oh, stop," Flash said, making a kissy noise. "You know you love me."

"Fuck you."

"Tempting, but no."

"What the fuck do you want?" Greg snapped, finally waking up properly.

"I need you to hack Phar-Scape again. I want to go in as well, and I can't do that without a cover."

"Okay, okay," Greg said, heading for his computer. "You're lucky that their shit is so piss poor I can literally do this in my sleep."

Flash followed Greg to the computer and watched him boot up the machine. Even though he was still yawning and rubbing his eyes, the lines of code streaked across the screen in blindingly fast-changing characters, with Greg's hands moving across the keys with an almost supernatural speed.

"I just realized something," Greg said. "There are no open positions at the company for you to take. You have to find another way to get in." He yawned. "Wake me when you figure it out."

Flashed growled low and menacingly, causing the computer guru to tense in his chair.

"Fine," Greg grumbled, "you owe me bigger than shit for this."

"Yeah, whatever," Flash said with a grin. He watched as the monitor displayed a list of company names. "What are those?"

"Vendors in Phar-Scape's accounting system. Maybe you can get access through one of them."

Flash saw a name he recognized. "What about that one?" His finger touched the screen.

Greg clicked around, bringing up another screen. "This invoice is from last week for construction work. Looks like they are building a parking garage next to the office building and doing some remodeling."

"Right," Flash blurted. "They are a construction company. I've seen their name at construction sites around town. And I can do that stuff."

"Seems fitting," Greg said as he typed away, then yawned and rubbed his face. "I've got you set up as a site supervisor. You'll have full access to all areas. This is a sensitive job, Flash. Are you sure you want to do this?"

"Of course, I'm sure. I'm not letting my mate go in there alone, especially since I just got tailed by a bunch of nasty shifters who were obviously after her."

"I just think that a job this delicate might be better suited to Slade," Greg said bluntly. Flash scoffed.

"Really? How do you figure?"

"Forgive me, Flash," Greg said, yawning. "But you're the impulsive type. You could blow your cover if someone stood in front of you for too long in the coffee line."

"I'm not that bad," muttered Flash.

"No? What about that bar fight where the guy took too long to line up the shot in darts, and you smashed a crystal pitcher of scotch over his head?"

Flash sighed. "I told you, he was holding that fucking dart for a whole ten minutes."

"My, what a crime," Greg said, laughing.

"Look, I can do this. I'm capable of holding my temper."

"Evidence to support this statement has yet to be found."

"Well, keep your eyes on me then, asshole," Flash snapped. "And I'll show you."

He'd been watching the screen as Greg added

him to the list of employees, paying vague attention, so he got an idea of how many people worked on the site and what their jobs were. When a name he recognized flickered on the screen, he reached over Greg's shoulder and slapped the keyboard.

"Hey, what the fuck?" Greg cried.

"My sentiments exactly," Flash muttered. He brought one hand slowly up to the screen and tapped it.

"Jenny Reynolds," he whispered.

"Slade's sister?" exclaimed Greg. Flash nodded slowly.

"What the fuck is Slade's kid sister doing on the construction crew?" Flash muttered. This complicated things badly. Not only did they have one more person to look out for, but now it might be Slade that completely lost his shit and blew their cover, all to protect his baby sister.

CHAPTER 12
CASSANDRA

Gray dawn light leaked into the room as Cassandra woke. She blinked slowly, wondering where she was. As she rolled over and felt Slade's warm body beside her, everything came back to her in a rush of sensory memory.

Slade. What the hell got into me last night?

He did, obviously.

Cass rolled over, turning away from him. The bed was soft, the sheets deliciously slick against her skin. She was so comfortable that she wanted to stretch out and sleep for another few hours.

Preferably while slowly fucking him in between naps.

As she listened to Slade's steady breathing, anxiety grew within her. Cassandra tried to come to grips with her own strange behavior, and all she could feel was an enduring sense of comfort and safety.

She waited for shame and regret to replace it. A horrific wave of embarrassment that would spur her out of this bed and send her running from him as fast as she could.

But it didn't come, even though she lay there until the gray light turned golden. As a rule, she did not have casual sex. She had never once in her life jumped into bed with a random guy. Surely, this was wrong, and it was only a matter of time before her emotions caught up and punished her for her moment of weakness.

Slowly, she turned over again. Warmth flooded her chest as she looked at Slade's sleeping face. She felt intense contentment and familiarity, not shame or regret. She didn't know how or why, but meeting these guys was not random, not at all.

It felt like it was meant to be, and that scared her even more. The only thing that stopped her from getting up and fleeing the bed was the sense she belonged here, right beside him.

With Flash on the other side of me.

Cass shivered with pleasure. If she'd never had sex with a random dude before, she certainly had never fucked two at the same time. She expected to be shocked by the very idea, but to her surprise, the only thing she felt was intense unbelievable lust.

The image of both of them wrapped around her, kissing her, touching her, pleasuring her, excited her so much that she writhed, pressing her thighs together. She was slick as the images swirled through her mind, making her gasp with desire.

Her body was sore in all the best places, and as she began to ache and throb, the pangs from last night's vigorous exertions turned into a deep, ravenous craving.

Cassandra gulped, taking a deep breath and holding it as she tried to calm herself. Her mind might be in conflict, but her heart and body had already decided. She wanted them ... both of them ... maybe more than she had ever wanted anything in her entire life.

She sat up quickly, looking for her clothes. There were things to do, and she had to put this aside, at least for now.

As she pulled the sheets down and swung her

legs to the floor, Slade muttered and reached out for her. His fingertips grazed her back as she stood and took two steps away from the bed.

"Good morning," he said.

"Morning," she answered, not turning. Cass looked around the room and saw her clothes were hurled in several different directions. She hurried to gather them, struggling to remember how they had gotten spread around as if a small hurricane had flown through the room.

Cassandra put her clothes on quickly, still not turning to face him. When Slade didn't say anything, she finally looked over, wondering if he was getting up.

He lay on the bed, the sheets puddled around his waist. A ray of sunlight angled from the nearby window, glazing his magnificent body with pale gold. He stretched, making his biceps bulge, then slowly sat up.

Cass realized she was staring and quickly looked away. Her eyes fell on Slade's trousers, and she grabbed them, tossing them to him.

"Here," she said in a sharp tone. "Let's get going. I'm betting Schindler has something for us by now."

"Okay," Slade said softly. He watched her with

tangible disappointment. Obviously, he'd been hoping for a quick bit of morning sex before they got back to business.

If you only knew what just went on in my head. I don't know if the poor guy would be turned on or traumatized.

When Slade said that he and Flash weren't jealous, Cass had not considered being with both at once. Now that she'd thought about it, the images wouldn't leave her brain. She stood there, a blush creeping up her neck to her cheeks as her nipples hardened and her pussy throbbed.

"We ready?" Slade asked. Cass realized that while she'd been lost in an erotic fantasy, he'd gotten up and was standing in front of her. She met his eyes and saw his tense expression. He seemed like he wanted to ask her something, and she didn't want to find out what it was.

Hey, babe, want to fuck my best friend and me at the same time?

Cass held in a groan and pressed her thighs together. It wasn't just the intensity of the sexual images that troubled her. It was the feeling that she had every right to think this way as if it were perfectly natural.

As if we are meant to be.

The idea scared her so much that she was finally able to banish her lust and stand up straight, clearing her throat. Finding happiness in love was completely impossible, and it didn't matter how good this felt ... sooner or later, they'd find out how hard she was to live with, and then they'd leave her just like everyone else did.

"Let's find Schindler," she said, hurrying to the door. She heard him hurry to catch up but didn't look behind her just in case she got caught in those soulful eyes again. He wanted to say something to her, and Cass had a pretty good idea of what it was going to be. At this point, all she wanted was to forget last night and get back on the case.

Out in the hall, they almost tripped over Mickey, who directed them to the kitchen for breakfast. Cass might want to deny the night of lovemaking, but she was still famished from the exertion. She grabbed a banana and strong coffee, still doing her best to avoid conversation with Slade.

"I wonder where our host is," Slade said, stirring his coffee. "Should we search him out?"

"It's still pretty early," she said, trying not to

notice the way his luscious lips wrapped around a sugary donut. "Maybe we should wait."

"I don't know. I say we should check the study."

"After you," she said, gesturing with her cup.

Cass followed Slade through the halls, trying not to watch his tight ass flexing under his fitted pants. The harder she tried to convince herself that being with both of these guys was wrong, the stronger her attraction became.

"Hello?" called Slade as he knocked on the open door of the study.

"Come through," Schindler said, waving them to his desk. Cass forcefully dragged her mind away from her lusty thoughts and sat across from Schindler, giving him her full attention.

"What did you find?" she asked.

Schindler stared at his readouts for a little longer, waving a finger at them as he flicked through the pages with his other hand.

"I'm trying to convince myself that this is not as bad as it looks," Schindler said. "I've run the numbers over and over again, and it keeps coming up the same."

"How bad is it?" Slade asked. "Poison? Mind control? Forced shape-shifting serum?"

Schindler shook his head. "Worse than all of that, I'm afraid."

"Worse?" Cass cried. "What in the hell could be worse?"

"As an antidepressant, this is probably the most effective drug I have ever seen," Schindler began. "Obviously, you want to encourage dopamine, serotonin, and endorphins, but the major issue is that when these are artificially elevated with drugs, it creates a rebound that is difficult to correct."

"English, please," Slade muttered. "I failed first-year science."

"I didn't," Cass snapped. "You're telling me this raises the mood permanently without side effects?"

"It might," Schindler said. "The information here isn't long-range. But the projections suggest that, yes, the state would be permanent with no downside. Quite fascinating, really. I'd like to see the readouts for what happens if someone was taken off it suddenly ... like most antidepressants, it's cumulative."

"So, it's actually good for you?" Cass asked in disbelief. "This drug is completely legit?"

"I didn't say that," Schindler said, his voice

firm. "There is a signature in this data that is not chemical. I couldn't understand it at first, but I've finally cracked it. This is why I had to run the numbers so many times."

"What is it?" Slade asked. Schindler sighed.

"There is an invocation in the chemical makeup of the drug. It's ingenious, really. The chemical compound puts the mind in a blissful, suggestible state. Even psychics with strong shields would be completely unguarded just from one dose of it. The chain that I could not identify is not chemical. It's a spell."

"A spell?" Cassandra echoed, beginning to understand why this drug was so dangerous.

"What kind of spell?" Slade asked.

"It's a summoning," Schindler replied. "It allows anyone with this drug in their system to be possessed."

Cass struggled to absorb the concept. She'd never heard of anything like this before. Possessing someone wasn't easy. If it was, demons would be overrunning the streets.

"So, the chemical compound makes the person happy and relaxed. Then there is a summoning spell literally carved into the chemical signature?"

"That's correct, yes," Schindler said, nodding.

"As I said, it's ingenious. Never seen anything like this before. The combination of chemistry and arcane magic is quite admirable."

"Well, if I find the person responsible, I'll bring them around so you can geek out together," Slade muttered. "That is if I don't kill them first."

Cassandra stared straight ahead, her eyes focused on nothing. Her life's work was to hunt and slay demons. Possession was the worst of all because often, killing the demon couldn't be done without also killing the host. She hated it when an innocent had to die.

Up to now, that was a scenario that hadn't happened very often. Getting the person into the right vulnerable state and calling the demon into them was a difficult process. The person had to be kept suggestible, too, in case they started to fight the demon.

Now, all of that was irrelevant. Upon taking one tiny pill, any person walking down the street could become a vessel for demons and their spawn. She thought of all the innocent souls who could be taken over and turned evil by this, fury and despair filling her in equal measure.

Then she thought of how large the demon

army could swell and how few hunters there were. If the cost of innocent lives wasn't enough, this pill could see the Earth easily overrun by her deadly enemies.

FLASH

Flash whistled merrily as he walked onto the parking garage construction site. Even though it wasn't necessary, he carried a small stack of cardboard tubes and wore a hard hat as an accompaniment to his well-tailored business suit.

The site was massive, with a crew on the ground floor working with cement mixers, massive pylons, and metal saws that spewed sparks across the concrete. He found the busy atmosphere thrilling and his only worry was that he'd give himself away by being too enthusiastic.

As he headed for the office building's front door, one of the workers hurried over to him. Flash tried to get around him, but the guy flagged him down.

"Hey, you're one of the bosses, right?"

"Yeah," Flash confirmed. "First day on-site, though, bud. What can I do for you?"

"Six of the guys on G crew blasted out a load-bearing pillar this morning by accident," he said. "We can repair it, but I figure you'd want to discipline the guys."

"Are they your crew?" Flash asked, thinking fast. This was exactly the kind of thing he was trying to stay out of. A new manager who fucked up proper procedure would be noticed immediately on his first day.

"Yes, they are, sir," the guy said. "Newbies. More muscle than good sense, I'd say."

"I tell you what," Flash said smoothly, "you do your best with them for now. I'll chat with the others and see what they want to do. You fixed the situation, didn't you? There have been no delays in the job?"

"No, sir, no delays. We're on schedule."

"Great! Take care of it then, and I'll get back to you."

He slipped past the guy and through the front

doors, congratulating himself on handling the situation. He wanted to get upstairs to the office areas where he was sure he'd find Cass, and he wanted to do it without getting into any more confrontations.

He took the elevator to the top floor and quickly realized his mistake. The place was filled with construction workers, not office employees. Looked like some remodeling was being done. It would have looked suspicious to push the button and go back down, so he strode purposefully out onto the floor and looked around with a cynical expression on his face.

In the open section of the space, a small crew smoothed wet cement over rebar. He turned to go, but one of the people in the crew looked familiar.

Is it Cass?

He was sure it wasn't, but his attention was taken all the same. After a minute of drawing a blank, he was ready to go over for a closer look, even if it risked his cover. Before he could, the girl turned, and he saw her face.

Jenny?

She was disguised in a wig and a pair of nerdy glasses, but it was definitely Slade's sister. Before she noticed him, Flash headed back to the elevator. Luckily, his status as a boss made everyone keep their heads down and ignore him.

He went down a few floors, finally coming to an area that looked like office space. There was no construction going on, just professional people in business suits setting up computers and moving files between cabinets.

Flash abandoned his cardboard tubes and hard hat, straightening his suit as he walked through the lines of desks. If there were dodgy deals going down, it would probably be here, somewhere. He hadn't gone far when a delicious scent fanned across his nostrils, making his mouth water.

Cass.

He followed the scent to a nearby corner office, where he found her going through a filing cabinet. She was dressed in a tight, knee-length skirt with a plain white blouse, her hair caught up in a neat bun. Flash leaned on the doorway, crossing his arms as he admired the view of her bent over.

He was able to enjoy the show for quite some time before she finally became aware of his presence. Tension streaked through her body, then she whipped around, shutting the door of the cabinet behind her.

"I'm so sorry, sir!" she cried. "I was just ... hey, wait ..."

Flash grinned, not moving a muscle as he watched her face switch from shock to fury.

"What the fuck are you doing here?" she muttered, looking around to make sure no one was watching.

Flash shrugged. "Just hanging out. How about you?"

"I'm looking for evidence," she whispered, hurrying over to him. "Are you seriously just standing there checking out my ass?"

"How could I not?" he murmured, reaching for her. "You were pointing it right at me. An excellent distraction for your cover, I might add."

"How dare you?" she hissed. "You'll blow my cover."

"What was that?" he asked, tilting his head toward her. "I'm hard of hearing. Did you just say you want to blow me?"

"Fuck you," she snapped. "This is serious."

"I know what I'm doing," he assured her. "I can handle this espionage thing."

Cass covered her face with her hand. "Yes, clearly, because starting a sexual harassment case on a personal assistant is awesome for your cover."

Flash shrugged. "It probably is. No one's noticed anything out of the ordinary so far."

"Just stay out of my way," Cass said angrily. She pushed past him, and for a moment, Flash was immersed in her wonderful scent. Something about it was even more intoxicating than before.

He took a deep breath and held it in the back of his nose. After a second, a smile of pure pleasure broke across his face.

She fucked Slade.

Even though she'd obviously showered and changed, he could still detect Slade's scent lingering on her skin. The idea turned him on so much that he had to wait for his cock to go down before following her out onto the main floor.

He noticed her straightaway on the other side of the office area. She was as far away from him as she could get, organizing a set of file folders. He walked toward her, completely forgetting why he was supposed to be there. He was so focused on her hot, luscious scent that everything else had ceased to matter.

"Excuse me," he said, pausing by her desk. "I thought I told you to work on the new files."

Flash pointed at a bunch of crates by the door. Cass clenched her jaw and glared at him.

"I'm working on this right now," she said. "I'll start on that soon."

"Are you talking back to me?" he snapped. "That's it. Get in my office now!"

Flash pointed at a nearby office, the only one that had blinds on its windows. Cass narrowed her eyes, shooting defiance at him. It would look strange to the others if she argued, so she got up and hurried to the corner office without a word.

"What the fuck do you think you're doing?" she hissed as he followed her inside and shut the door behind them. Flash ignored her for a second while he closed the blinds.

"I'm disciplining my wayward employee," he said, shaking his head. "If only you had followed orders, you wouldn't be in this position."

"Flash!" she snapped, trying to keep her voice low. "I don't know what you think you're doing, but we don't have time for it."

Flash stepped toward her until their bodies were inches apart. He smelled her arousal rising on a hot current of air that wafted from between her breasts. He took a deep breath and held it, letting the scent of her mixed with Slade's roll around on the back of his tongue.

He looked into her eyes and saw her pupils dilate. He sensed the heat in her body increase at exactly the same time. He was betting that she'd completely forgotten what she was saying.

"What?" he muttered, leaning close to her. "What were you saying?"

"Flash," she mumbled. "I can't …"

Flash almost moaned aloud as her scent suddenly became stronger and sharper. She was powerfully aroused, and there was no denying it. He reached for her, wrapping one arm around her waist and pulling her skirt up with his other hand.

"Flash, no," she whispered. "Someone will see."

Flash licked her neck, teasing her earlobe with the tip of his tongue. At the same time, he slid his hand between her thighs and buried his fingers in her hot, throbbing pussy.

"You're ready for me," he breathed, kissing her neck. "You want me so much, you can't even think."

"Flash," she whispered, her voice low and rough. He didn't give her a chance to say anything else. He pressed his lips to hers, opening her mouth with his tongue and searching for hers as his fingers slipped past her panties to find her clit.

Cass writhed in his arms, moaning so loudly he had to keep his mouth over hers. He rubbed her clit, struggling against her underwear as it twisted around his hand. With a hard, violent twist, he tore it off and dropped to his knees.

Cass pulled up her skirt, backing to brace herself on the desk. Flash moaned as he pushed her knees apart and dove under the skirt to press his lips to her clit.

He heard her cry out, a short, sharp sound that she muffled before it could become a scream. Flash's hands tightened on her thighs as he shoved his tongue deep inside her and forced her legs even farther apart.

She leaned back on the desk, bracing her hands behind her as she let him push her knees apart, opening so he could pleasure her with his tongue. Flash moaned softly as he lapped at her, loving the way she responded to his touch.

The only thing that would make this better was Slade being here.

He imagined his best friend behind Cass,

working her breasts or pleasuring himself in her throat while he brought her to climax with his tongue, over and over. The urge to trap her between the two of them and fuck her at the same time overwhelmed him, and Flash let out a loud moan that rang around the room.

She tensed against him, and he knew she was worried someone might hear. He should be, too, but his fantasies were running loose, and he couldn't rein them in. Flash stood suddenly, grabbing Cass's shoulders and kissing her hard.

She trembled in his arms, moaning into his mouth. Her breath hissed in and out of her, and she trembled with need. Flash's cock was so hard he felt like he was going to tear right out of his fly.

He stepped back, pulling Cass with him. He turned her around, shoving her over the desk while he pulled up her skirt. With a sharp yank, he got his own pants undone and grabbed her hips, ramming his cock into her.

Cass was flat against the desk, her hands wrapped around the edge so hard that her knuckles were white. Flash held her hips tightly in his hands, and his cock shoved into her pussy as far as it could go. As her inner muscles clenched and spasmed around his hard, throbbing cock, he gasped as the pleasure sang through him.

All other sensations and thoughts were banished from his mind. There was only Cass, all over him, in his mouth, on his lips, and wrapped around his cock.

CHAPTER 14

CASSANDRA

Cass pressed her lips together, desperately trying to stop herself from crying out. She clung to the desk while Flash pounded her, his hard cock slamming into her with long, fast strokes. The pleasure pulsed through her, making her lean forward and cling tighter to the desk to urge him on.

He reached out and clamped a hand down on her shoulder, pressing his body against hers and freezing in place. She felt a shudder run through him that echoed in her own body as if they had truly become one.

For a moment, both were still, then an enormous orgasm rushed through her. It came from deep inside and resonated through every nerve in her body. She turned her face against the hardwood of the desk and covered her mouth to stop from crying out.

Flash pulled out as the spasms began to subside, and his hands pressed against her ass cheeks. She whimpered as his tongue slid into her hot, slick pussy. He teased her with his lips, delved deeply inside, and slowly brought her to orgasm again.

Staying quiet as the pleasure shot through her was the hardest thing Cass had ever done. She trembled and moaned into her hand, completely senseless with desire. When Flash stood and lifted her, turning her toward him, she was loose and pliant in his arms.

He kissed her, holding her against his body. Her skirt was pulled up over her hips, and his pants were around his ankles, his solid cock pressed against her. As they kissed, she squirmed, teasing herself.

Flash reached down and rubbed her clit with his fingers, exciting her with long, firm strokes. She gasped and trembled, letting her head fall back as he kissed her even more deeply.

Cass thrust her hips more forcefully toward him, her knees climbing his thighs. Flash reached around, grabbed her ass, and pressed against her. She clung to his shoulders and writhed, trying to join them together.

If only Slade were here.

She moaned, trying to hold her voice in. The idea of Slade behind her while Flash trapped her body between them was so overwhelming she felt dizzy. When Flash wrapped his hands around her thighs and hoisted her up, she relaxed in his arms, opening her hips, so her body joined with his in one quick movement.

Flash turned, still holding her hips and waist. She cried out when he slammed her against the nearby wall, literally biting her tongue to hold it in. He bent his head to her breasts, and Cass fumbled with the buttons, finally opening the blouse and pulling her bra out of the way.

Flash's hands stayed braced on her ass while his hips kept her against the wall. Cass's hands lazily traced across his shoulders, eventually finding their way to the back of his neck, where she clung to him with shaking fingers.

Through the mess of bra straps and the edges

of the blouse, Flash found her nipples, pulling them with his lips before nipping with his teeth. Cass twisted against the wall, a lump of lust without any thought or control.

Another orgasm built. Flash hoisted her into a better position, his fingers digging into her thighs as he started to ram her in long, even strokes. Cass leaned her head back, going limp in his arms as he pounded her.

Flash thickened inside her, and his strokes became faster and harder. Cass held on to him, whimpering as another tremendous orgasm shook through to her bones. As her hot, throbbing pussy clenched around him, Flash's cock spurted deep inside her.

He shuddered, gasping as he tried to regain control of himself. They looked into each other's eyes, and both of them smiled, giggling a little. Flash stroked her cheek and kissed her softly. She opened her thighs again, thrusting her breasts against him. Cass felt him getting excited again, and her own passion intensified in anticipation.

Then, a sudden noise crackled through her with so much force she felt like she might pass out. Flash grabbed her with both hands and twirled them around the room, shoving them both into a nearby coat closet.

I have to admire his footwork since he's still got his pants around his ankles.

They fell into the dark space and pulled the door to, but with the door not latching, behind them just as two men entered the room. Cass's heart pumped so fast that she saw black spots in front of her eyes. Holding her breath, so she didn't pant like a dying dog made her ears ring. She blinked hard, swallowing her shock and surprise so she could calm down.

"Where's the spreadsheet for Jenkins?"

"In the updated file."

"Great."

Cass was able to let her breath out in a long, slow rush. It didn't seem like the guys coming into the room had noticed them. She caught Flash's eye, and he nodded, holding a finger to his lips.

She peered out through the narrow opening in the doorway, trying to get a look at the guys. She couldn't hide her shock when she saw it was Henry Crenshaw and Kent Edwards.

Just the guys I've been hoping to see ... at the worst possible time.

"Is the holdup in production taken care of?" Edwards asked, sitting at the desk.

"Yeah, I had to replace several of the humans," Crenshaw said, sitting across from him and booting up the computer. "The hardest thing at the moment is maintaining the outward operations so the entire thing has credit. The media is becoming a bitch to hide from."

"Shit, who would have guessed running a fake company could be so difficult."

"You said it," Henry agreed, tapping the mouse. "These financial documents are an absolute pain in the ass. Damn investigative reporters."

"Hopefully, we won't have to keep this up much longer."

"We're on schedule for the thirty-first."

Cass leaned forward, trying to get a better look. She could barely move because she was still trapped in the tangled bra and blouse, not to mention her skirt pulled up around her waist. She didn't dare try to put her clothes back on properly, not with those two sitting so close.

Can they smell me? Fuck, I hope not.

She was pretty sure if they noticed any smell at all, it would more than likely be Flash. It was very likely that their overconfidence meant they simply weren't paying attention.

"It was a good idea," Edwards said. "Perfect way to get everyone involved."

"No one can resist free money," Crenshaw said, a satisfying note to his voice. "Everyone wants something for nothing."

"Even you?"

"Don't be funny. It just makes you look pathetic."

"Fuck you. Hurry up."

"Emailing it to Jenkins now."

"Let's get out of here. All this remodeling shit is giving me a headache."

"Agreed," Crenshaw said. Even though Edwards got up, Crenshaw took a minute to go through the desk drawer, pulling out a thick cigar and lighting it with a match. Cass sighed with relief. It would make it almost impossible for both of them to smell her, even if she was dripping with lust. She didn't know what kind of powers these guys possessed ... she assumed they weren't ordinary humans ... but if a cigar could mess up Slade's sense of smell, it could do it to anyone.

Cass watched the men as they headed for the door. She sensed a thick, dark aura over one or both of them. It unsettled her because the demon presence had to be incredibly strong for it to be so foreboding.

And completely evil.

She watched them leave the office, wishing she could tail them and fully investigate the demonic presence. It could complicate things dramatically if she underestimated these guys. It wasn't just a dodgy pill they were dealing with here ... it could be a very high-level demon.

"Are they gone?" she whispered, watching Flash's face. He had his head tilted to the side, listening to the footsteps of the men.

"They're getting in the elevator now," Flash said quietly. Cass breathed a sigh of relief and stood to straighten her clothes.

"Aww," Flash muttered. "Don't go putting all my toys away. I wasn't done playing with them yet."

"Ha-ha," Cass muttered, slapping his hand away. "We came close enough to fucking up the mission today. We don't need a round two."

"How about round three or four?" Flash asked, holding her arms gently and pulling her against him. "It might be even better if I could tag in another team member, like my best pal Slade."

Cass felt the strength go out of her as Flash kissed her. She sagged against his strong chest, wondering if she'd heard him correctly or if she was so fixated on her fantasies she was hearing what she wanted to hear.

"Quit it," she muttered, pushing him away. "We have to get moving. One of those guys is possessed by an extremely strong demon. Well, they both could be. It's difficult to tell. The bottom line is, I need intel on this and fast."

"Yeah, okay. They said they had the thing planned for Halloween?"

Cass nodded. "The day when the veil is at its thinnest."

"What? That's real?"

Cass grinned. "Yes. Don't get me wrong, there are other days, and you can push through the veil in lots of other ways too. But All Hallows Eve, the day of the dead, is the most effective time to conjure ... and to be possessed."

"So, you think whatever is going down, it's happening on Halloween?"

"Yeah," she said. "Got no idea how free money fits in, though. What is he going to do? Offer up free antidepressants to anyone who gets their number called?"

Flash laughed softly. "You never know. What do you think we should do?"

Cass looked at him, seeing sincerity on his face. It pleased her that he genuinely cared about her opinion. It made up for him suddenly appearing in the middle of her covert mission.

"Well, we have to figure out what Crenshaw is up to, and we need to do it quickly," she said. "We're running out of time, and so many innocent people could get hurt by this. Maybe we should stake out his favorite places and shake down anyone in his chain of command."

"We could," Flash agreed.

"This might be a good place to start," Cass said. "Although I haven't seen him being particularly chummy with anyone here at the office."

"I love your ideas," Flash said. "But it's not my style. I think we should go for a more direct approach."

"Oh?" Cass asked, afraid that she knew exactly what Flash was going to say.

"We just nab the guy," Flash muttered, slamming a fist into his palm. "Then we force him to tell us everything he knows."

Cass shook her head, enjoying his impulsive nature but wondering if she'd be able to get through to him. Full-on confrontation should be their last choice, especially if Crenshaw was possessed. There was just too much that could go wrong, and for the first time in her life, Cassandra actually had something worth living for.

SLADE

Slade waited in the deep shadows in the corner of an alley. He was not far from Jenny's favorite coffee shop, and he'd been coming here for days hoping to run into her.

No matter what the high-spirited little minx was up to, he was sure she'd be back here sooner or later. This shop carried a rare blend of coffee beans that were roasted a certain way, and Jenny said she never had her morning coffee unless she had it here.

The place was fairly busy, with a lot of people coming and going. Slade kept his eyes on the doors and stretched against the alley wall, trying not to look too conspicuous. He had one of his super fragrant cigars in his hand, curling out little spirals of smoke. If anyone noticed him, they'd just assume he was trying to have a smoke in peace.

Or I'm a drug dealer lurking in the alley waiting for my connection.

Slade laughed softly. It would serve him right if the cops came along. He'd probably get arrested for stalking his own sister.

He looked down at the ground for a second, amused at his own antics. He was getting so worried about Jenny that he was ready to scour every inch of the street for her scent. All he wanted was to protect her, and it seemed as if the situation was getting more dangerous by the minute.

If she's okay, why doesn't she just tell me?

Even though Slade was looking right at the front windows, it took him a minute to realize that a slight girl with flaming red hair was in the doorway of the coffee shop. He felt the recognition strike him like a bolt of pure lightning as he realized it was definitely his sister.

Slade jogged across the road, tossing away his cigar. Instead of rushing into the shop, he waited by the door, just to the side. He didn't want to give her a chance to see him and then sneak out a back way.

He felt her presence before he saw her. Even

though his sense of smell was a bit whacked from the cigar, he could still smell her. When she shoved the door open and walked past him, her scent smacked him right in the face. He lurked behind her for a few seconds, watching her tilt her head back for a big sip from the tall cup.

"Enjoying your coffee?" he asked casually. Jenny jumped, barely holding on to the cup as she spun around to face him.

"Slade," she muttered.

"Yes, Slade. Your brother. Your guardian. The guy that's meant to keep you safe. You can't even answer my calls?"

"Look, Slade," Jenny said, sighing. "I don't want to do this with you right now. I've got places to be."

Slade scowled, feeling his irritation turning into full-blown anger.

"You ran away from home without even telling me. All your friends refused to tell me where you'd gone. You're taking too many risks ... where are you even sleeping?"

Jenny had regained her composure and took a long sip from her cup.

"If I tell you where I'm staying, you're just going to show up there and junk up the place. I don't need you making my friends uncomfortable."

"Excuse me?"

"Do you dare to deny that's exactly what you'd do? I can see it all now. You'd show up and interrogate everyone right before you bagged, tagged, and dragged me home."

"That's exactly my plan," Slade growled. "How am I supposed to look after you if you insist on doing such dangerous things?"

"You have no fucking clue what I'm doing," Jenny snapped. "Will you stop treating me like a child? I'm nineteen, for fuck's sake. I didn't run away from home. I moved out. It's a pretty common thing for a young adult to do."

Slade absorbed the words in cold silence. He understood her words, but they didn't measure up against that morning he'd woken and found her gone. The terror he'd felt as he ran around the house screaming her name came back to him with visceral impact.

He'd been absolutely sure she'd been kidnapped or killed. His mind automatically went to the worst possible place. Flash had calmed him and showed him some of her things were missing.

He had still struggled to believe that she'd simply left without telling him.

Slade noticed a few people in the coffee shop watching them, so he gestured to the corner of the alley, and Jenny nodded, sighing. Slade almost grabbed her when she rolled her eyes to give her a hard shake.

"Jenny! Do you understand how terrified I was when I woke up and found you gone?"

That gave her some pause. He saw the look of regret flash across her face.

"I'm sorry, Slade. I really am. But I knew I'd never get out of there if I told you. You'd probably lock me up if you couldn't argue me into a standstill."

"You might be right there," he muttered.

"You're too overprotective," Jenny said in a reasonable tone. "You need to trust me. I'm perfectly capable of looking after myself."

Slade sighed, looking at the ground for a few seconds as he gathered himself.

"What about your undercover work?"

"What?" Jenny asked, the color draining from her face.

Slade sensed her uneasiness, which was not

quite fear but definitely rising anxiety. "I know what you're doing at Phar-Scape."

"Do you?" Jenny snapped, hurling her coffee into a nearby bin. "You can't possibly. How do you even know I was there?"

"Not only have we had our own operations going on there, but Flash also confirmed it for me. He saw you there. What the fuck are you doing in such a dangerous place?"

"Construction work," Jenny said casually. "Putting steel girders into concrete, smoothing grout, re-designing plumbing systems. You know, the usual."

"Will you be serious," Slade snapped. "Did you know the company was dirty when you applied there, or is this your idea of a good first job?"

Jenny sighed. "I knew they were bad."

"What the fuck?" Slade cried. "You're admitting to this? Why the hell are you doing this?"

Jenny regarded him with a calm, even gaze.

"I have my own interests there. Sorry, Slade, but there are things I need to do. Flash isn't the only shifter to go missing, you know. Phar-Scape is involved. We know that much."

"So, your best idea is to jump straight into the fucking fire?"

"Yes," Jenny said coolly. "I was doing a good job of it until you showed up. If you tracked me and Flash saw me at work, that means my cover is compromised. I'm in more danger than I was before because of you."

"Hold up," Slade said, shaking his head. "I'm here to protect you, not hurt you. It doesn't matter if your cover is compromised. You're not going back there."

"Excuse me?" Jenny asked very softly.

"My mind is made up. You can come along quietly or be dragged. If you force me to lock you up, that's on you."

Jenny stared at him in complete disbelief.

"I can't believe I'm hearing this," Jenny whispered. "Do you really think you're protecting me?"

A horrible fear rose in him. The cauldron of his grief and doubt was manifesting into rage. He pointed it at everything that opposed him, even his sister.

I can't lose you! I have to keep you safe!

Jenny hadn't moved, but she had a look of urgency about her as if she could feel danger. Slade was so furious and frightened that he reached out and grabbed her arm.

His mind was full of horrifying images. He

didn't know exactly what was being done to the kidnapped shifters. Flash had remembered a few things, but not enough for Slade to know exactly what happened.

That didn't matter. His imagination was very effective at generating horrible, nightmarish images. He saw his sister strapped to a stretcher as men in white coats stuck needles into her. He saw her chained to a wall and tortured. He saw her forced to shift and then run down and torn apart by hunting dogs.

He blinked hard, coming back to the present moment. His hand tightened on her arm. He was almost frantic with fear.

Jenny stared at him with wide, shining eyes. She stood completely still as if she were a stone statue.

"Slade. I'm going to tell you once. Take your hand off me."

He wanted to. On some deep level, he was aware that his hold on her was unhealthy and bordering on harmful. The last thing he wanted was to hurt her, but he had no choice. He could hurt her, or their enemies would. There was no middle ground.

"No," he said, tightening his hold. "You have to

come with me. We can talk more about this …
when we get home."

Slade tugged on her arm, trying to drag her
down the street. To his surprise, Jenny dug in her
heels and refused to budge. He looked back at her
in confusion.

"Jenny?" Slade asked, his eyes traveling up and
down her slight frame. She looked exactly the
same as she always had, his skinny kid sister.

How did she get so strong?

He tugged on her arm again. Jenny set her
mouth in a firm line and shook her head.

Slade leaned back, ready to put the full force of
his body into the next shove. He was taking her
home whether she liked it or not.

To his surprise, Jenny's form flowed under his
hand as she shifted. He was so shocked that he let
go. The wolf twisted in the air, turning and snapping at him. Her jaws clamped over his forearm,
and her teeth went through his skin. She shook
her head back and forth, tearing open a huge,
ragged wound.

Slade screamed and staggered backward.
Jenny barked once, then turned and bolted down
the alley. Slade leapt toward her, shifting as he
ran. She had a head start on him, and he was

injured. Still, he had no intention of letting her get away.

Slade ran down the alley as fast as he could, watching Jenny's flashing form ahead of him. The alley turned a sharp corner and then became a long straight path with nowhere to hide. Even though he couldn't catch up, he was maintaining his pace. She wouldn't be able to get out of sight.

As he ran, his leg tried to heal. It was difficult when he was exerting himself so much, and he was leaving a decent trail of blood.

I can't believe she fucking bit me.

He shouldn't have tried to physically force her, but couldn't she understand how serious the situation was? What if she was killed? He would never forgive himself.

He kept his eyes focused on the fluffy plume of her tail as she darted ahead of him. He would heal, and he'd catch up to her. Then he'd make her understand, and she'd go home with him and forget this nonsense.

CHAPTER 16

SLADE

A red haze covered Slade's vision, accompanied by the steady thump of his strong heartbeat and the rush of air in his lungs. His leg still hurt, and his entire body was screaming for him to stop.

He growled in frustration and tried to run even faster, looking ahead for the fluffy tail that beckoned him forward.

To his shock, the alley was empty.

Slade stopped, looking from left to right. The alley went straight in front of him. There were no turns.

Where the fuck did she go?

Slade prowled forward, each step slow and light. His leg healed, and his breathing and heart rate slowed, diminishing the red haze that wavered across his gaze.

Then he noticed a narrow side street leading between two buildings. He spun around, quickly looking into other nooks beside apartment doors. There were tiny passages everywhere that connected to side streets, and Slade had totally missed all of them.

She could be anywhere by now.

Slade growled and shook his head. He walked over to the edge of the street and lay down, stretching his nose out on his paws. He whined a little as he watched his leg finish healing.

He was so full of fear and anxiety, as well as being completely exhausted, he literally couldn't think straight. His mind struggled to deal with the situation, and he kept returning to the fact he was going home without Jenny.

Sorrow built in his breast, sending longing streaking through his blood. The emotion became something else in his wolf heart, something beyond human comprehension. He tilted his head back and howled at the sky, a lament to his loneliness and his failure.

I've let you down, Mother. I couldn't keep her safe.

Now she's out there. I don't know where, and anything could happen to her.

The horrible images flew through his mind again. Slade struggled against them, trying to tell himself that none of it was true. These things had happened, though, to other shifters, including his best friend. It could happen to his sister too.

Why can't she see that?

Emptiness rose in him again, but he couldn't sit here all day and howl. He was bound to be noticed. Slowly, he got up, testing his paw. The wound had closed, even though his leg was still sore. He had no desire to turn back and find his clothes; his wolf was comforting in his current state.

As he loped through the side streets, his fear for Jenny was replaced by his need to get home. He had to see his best friend and his mate. They were the only ones who could soothe him.

I hope they're home from the dodgy job. I couldn't handle it if both of them were caught.

It took some time to run through the streets, but he was glad for it. Running and feeling his body stretching and pushing past endurance comforted him. By the time he got to the house, his mind was wiped clean of fear and doubt.

There was still plenty of rage, though. The wolf had covered the fear and replaced it with the need for violence. His mother's eyes lurked in his memory, berating him for not being strong enough to look after Jenny. Slade couldn't be free of it or from guilt.

He shifted on the doorstep and charged inside, slamming the door behind him. When he walked into the main living room, he saw Cass sitting on the couch, watching him with alarm. Flash was at the bar making himself a drink and barely looked up.

"My man," Flash muttered, pouring from three different bottles into a tall glass. "What can I get you?"

"A straight jacket and a butterfly net," Slade snapped. "Then the location of my sister."

Flash looked up in surprise. Cass laughed softly. "Yeah, family can drive you mad, I guess."

Slade turned to look at her. His eyes were cold. "I'm not joking. I'm going to run her down and throw her in a locked room."

Cass frowned, obviously trying to figure out his elaborate joke. "You can't be serious?" she said.

Flash hurried around the bar and put a glass of bourbon in Slade's hand. "Drink up, brother,"

Flash said. "It's human stuff, but it is finely aged. It'll calm you a bit."

Slade threw the alcohol down his throat in one gulp. He shook as the high emotions tried to settle against his raging hot blood.

"I found her, okay? I questioned her. She won't tell me what she's doing or why, and she won't stop. She fucking bit me. Like, actually tore into me."

"Whoa," Flash muttered.

"I mean, what kind of response is she expecting after running away and refusing to tell me where she went?" Slade cried, exasperated.

"How old is she again?" Cass asked, frowning.

"Only nineteen," Slade said, shaking his head. "Poor kid. She has no idea what she's doing. I've got to bring her home and keep her here until I can figure out what to do."

"When I was nineteen, I was kicking demon butt on the streets," Cass said, shrugging. "Just sayin'. If she's your sister, she's probably a badass. Why are you so worried?"

"Because she's a fucking kid!" Slade yelled. Flash turned to Cass, a worried look on his face.

"Look, you don't know Jenny, okay? She's super spoiled and does things just to get to Slade.

She doesn't know how dangerous the situation is or that she's putting all of us at risk."

"Okay," Cass muttered as if she had more to say but thought better of it.

"She'll be back at Phar-Scape soon, I imagine," Slade said. "Have we got a plan?"

"Yep," Flash said proudly. "We're going to get ahold of Crenshaw and squeeze him until he squeals."

Slade looked at them both with a flat expression. "That's it?"

"That's it," Flash said with a smarmy grin.

"That's fucking stupid," Slade growled.

"Hey," Flash protested. "Don't act like I don't know what I'm doing."

"You don't know what you're doing," Slade shot back.

"Take it easy," Cass said. "We've got time to flesh out the plan."

Slade covered his face with his palm. "Whatever the fuck you guys have got happening, I have no choice but to be a part of it. My kid sister is there, and she's not going to stop. If I want to keep her safe, this is what I have to do."

"Nice to know you have so much confidence in me, bro," Flash muttered.

"What's the first step? Are we just going to jump on Crenshaw when he gets out of his limo somewhere?"

"There's a mixer tonight," Cass said. "Big bash for the night before Halloween. We think it might be a good opportunity to isolate Crenshaw."

"It might," Slade said, thinking. "Is anyone going to pay much attention to us? I want to get in too."

"That's cool," Cass said. "I've got Flash an invite. You can go as my plus one."

"Good," Slade said, nodding. He was relieved that he'd be there to protect his mate and his kid sister.

"What are you going to wear?" Flash asked, gesturing at Cassandra. She laughed at his doubtful expression.

"I don't know. I don't think I have a dress for this type of occasion."

"Then let us take you out," Slade said. "I don't want our cover in jeopardy even slightly."

Cass agreed, and Slade went to clean up and change. As soon as he was done, he ushered them to the car, and they drove to the nearest mall.

While Cass looked at dresses, Flash wandered off to check out some stores. Slade found himself relaxing as Cass tried on outfits. He could tell she wasn't used to being treated like this, and she was enjoying herself.

I'll see Jenny tonight if she's at the party. Then I can see that she's safe. Maybe even talk her out of this nonsense.

"Okay, Slade," Cass said, coming out of the changing room in a slinky red number. Slade gasped at the length of exposed thigh as well as how the crimson set off her pale skin and golden hair.

"You can pick out as many as you want," Slade said. "Don't think about just tonight. I want you to have all sorts of nice things."

"Where am I going to wear it?" she said, laughing. "Demon hunting? Should I pair it with combat boots?"

"If you like," Slade said, grinning. "I like the look."

Cass turned and disappeared into the stalls. Shortly after that, he heard her cursing up a storm.

"What is it?" he called, going to the door of her fitting room, hoping no one was in the next space.

"I can't get this zipper," she muttered.

"May I come in?"

"Sure."

Slade pushed the door open and saw Cass struggling to reach a zipper stopped at the midpoint of her back. Even though she was trying to reach it from both directions, she couldn't quite catch it in either hand. Slade took a moment to admire the short, sequined black dress. He hoped she'd pick this one for tonight.

"Here," he said, "let me."

Cass lifted her hair, and Slade grabbed the edge of the zipper and slowly sealed the back of the dress, admiring her soft, pale skin as he did. Her scent enveloped him, and Slade gulped, almost drunk on her natural perfume.

"What do you think?" she asked, turning. "Is it too short?"

"No," Slade muttered. "No way."

He couldn't take his eyes off her curves, hugged by the black, lacey fabric. The sequins glinted like subtle stars scattered across a dark, moody sky. Her long, silky thighs were exposed, as were her well-toned arms. The neckline plunged into a modest V-shape that framed her cleavage perfectly.

"You look stunning," he whispered, his mouth brick dry.

"I get that," Cass giggled. "But I don't think I could walk down the street like this."

"Why not?" Slade asked, baffled. "You're a beautiful woman. What could you be ashamed of?"

"Not ashamed," Cass said. "How could I fight in this?" She tried to kick to prove her point, and the dress crawled up her hip, exposing her ass. She laughed. "I'm assuming I'll be in high heels too. So, I'll be a sweet, juicy piece of eye candy incapable of defending myself."

"I'll defend you," Slade said, reaching for her hand. "I'll never let anything happen to you."

Cass smiled, reaching out to stroke his hair. He pulled her close, tightening his arms around her waist. When their lips met, his fears and doubts faded just a little. Cass squirmed against him, and the dress slid up her hips to her waist. He smelled her wet heat. Without thinking about what he was doing, he pressed her against the wall with one hand and reached down between her legs with the other to rub her clit.

"No panties," he whispered, smiling.

Cass shrugged. "I was planning on getting some that matched the dress when I finally picked one."

"I approve," he muttered. "Except about finding new underwear. I'd like you to stay like this at all times."

Cass giggled, the laughter getting stuck in her throat as Slade's rough fingertips teased her, rubbing deeper into her throbbing pussy. Slade buried his head against her shoulder, knowing that this was the only thing that could ever heal him.

Cassandra.

She was mystery, grace, fire, and comfort all at once, and he couldn't get enough of her.

CHAPTER 17

CASSANDRA

Cass leaned back against the wall, enjoying the thrill of possible discovery mixed with the lust that flooded through her as Slade rubbed her clit with strong, rough fingers. She giggled as he pushed her even harder against the wall, wondering what they would do if someone happened to walk in.

She struggled to hold in her breathy moans, gasping in between kisses as Slade pleasured her. Just as she began to shiver in anticipation, Slade went to his knees and started eating her, making her let out a loud, sharp cry.

In a nearby stall, someone jumped and made a sound of surprise. Cass bit her lip and looked down at Slade, who winked at her as he dove down to tease her with his tongue.

"We should stop," she murmured.

"Don't look at me," Slade muttered. "I'm not the one making all the noise."

Cassandra tried to protest, but Slade was stroking her pussy with his tongue, leaving her breathless and trembling with excitement. He seemed to know exactly how much pressure to give her clit before he moved his lips and tongue to caress her lower folds.

She closed her eyes, holding in her moans with extreme difficulty. Slade increased his pace, and Cass felt the orgasm roaring through her, making her slap the wall with frustration as she tried to stay quiet.

She leaned heavily against the mirror, her legs practically useless when Slade stood and kissed her very gently. His hands slid along her hips, pushing the short dress out of the way as he pressed her to the wall.

"We can't," she breathed, beyond rational thought but still clinging to some scrap of socially accepted behavior.

"We can't what?" he asked innocently. He

reached down and opened his pants, and her breath rasped through her throat as her arousal increased. "Can't do this?" he said with a grin. Just as Cassandra tried to speak, Slade shoved his hips forward and his hard cock pressed against her slick pussy.

She groaned, not even bothering to try to stay quiet. She burned from head to toe, and the craving within her would not be denied.

"Don't stop," she whispered in his ear. "Please, don't stop."

Slade grinned and wrapped his hands around her ass, lifting her and bracing them both against the wall. Slade joined them together in one long, fast thrust from his hips, his cock slamming straight into her wet folds.

Cass let out a long, drawn-out wail. She bit her lip hard, shaking her head as she tried to stay quiet. Slade covered her mouth with his own, stroking her tongue and pressing his hot lips to hers. Cass relaxed, leaning back against the wall as he started to thrust.

With every sharp movement of his hips, Cassandra banged against the flimsy barrier. She had a sudden image of them actually falling through it. Her cries of lust turned into giggles of glee as she pictured herself and her lover landing at the feet of some poor, innocent shopper. At the same time, the entire fitting room came down around them.

Slade paused, his hips pressed hard against her, looking into her eyes. Cass reached up and stroked his cheek, feeling incredibly relaxed and tender toward him. There was a connection here that she couldn't fathom, something that sang deep in her cells. Being with him felt right.

Being with Flash feels right too. How could I choose between them?

Easy. Don't.

Slade gripped her thighs, his tight fingertips returning her to the present moment. She blinked, letting herself fall straight into Slade's gaze. As he swelled inside her, she saw the look in his eyes change. He was fiercely dominant, but as he came closer to his climax, she saw an incredible vulnerability locked inside his soul.

Not locked now. It's open for me.

The realization that he was opening to her electrified her desire, making her moan and writhe against the wall. Slade kissed her again, keeping his lips clamped on hers as he increased his pace.

Cass came in a flooding rush, clamping her legs to his sides and gripping his shoulders as the climax seared her blood. Deep inside, she felt Slade's body pumping against hers. If she hadn't had her lips locked on his, she definitely would have screamed.

He held her against the wall for a few minutes, their foreheads together. When she looked into his eyes, they were dark with emotion. Cass ran a hand down his cheek, smiling. He grinned back.

"Do you think anyone heard us?" he whispered.

Cass giggled. "I think everyone heard us," she joked.

Slade moved back a step, gently putting her feet back on the ground. "Do they have security cameras in here?" Slade asked, looking around.

"They do," she said. "I don't know if they would have caught us, though."

"Wouldn't security be kicking us out?" Slade asked, puzzled.

"I don't think anyone would dare knock on this door," Cass said, giggling. She let herself recover for a few minutes, not rushing to get dressed or leave the cubicle. It was a special moment for just the two of them, a wild exercise of abandon she didn't want to forget.

They cleaned up and finally prepared to bolt from the changing area, Cass's stack of dresses over Slade's arm. They sneaked to the door, peeking around the edge to see if they were being watched, then made a run for it back to the women's section.

"There you are," Flash growled as he approached through the rows of neatly hung dresses. "What the hell took you so long?"

Cass blushed, and Slade winked. Flash laughed softly.

"Fair enough," he said. "Did you pick a dress, at least?"

Slade held up one arm. "More than one. Can you take these? I need to check my phone."

"Sure thing," Flash said, reaching out for the stack of dresses. Slade immediately pulled out his phone and stared at the screen, disappointment slowly breaking across his features. Cass stood next to Flash, watching Slade with some concern.

She watched his fingers dance across the screen as he checked a few different apps, then locked the phone and put it back in his pocket. He took two steps away from them, then pulled the phone out again to look forlornly at the locked screen.

"What the fuck?" she muttered. "Should I be insulted? We were just having mind-blowing sex. Now he's tied to his phone."

"Don't take it personally," Flash said. "He's probably feeling guilty that he indulged when he still has no idea where Jenny is."

"Oh," Cass said. "The nineteen-year-old sister, right?"

"Yeah, that's right."

Cass watched Slade put his phone away, then get it out again. She frowned.

"Is he okay? Like, actually?"

Flash sighed. "Look, he's got a good reason to be a bit paranoid. He lost everyone he loves, and he thinks he's going to let everyone down if he doesn't keep her safe. He can't stand the idea of losing her."

"I get that," Cass said. "But if he doesn't loosen that stranglehold he's got on her, he will definitely lose her."

"Yeah," Flash shrugged. "I know. I thought he'd ease off a bit as she got older, but it seems to have gotten worse."

"I'd like to meet her," Cass said.

"You might have," Flash answered. "She's undercover on the site at Phar-Scape."

"Oh, right," Cass nodded. "I doubt it, though. Trust me, Slade doesn't want me chatting with his sister. We are going to come down on the same side. And I mean against him."

"I don't think he could take that," Flash said seriously. "I know he wants to protect you just as much. He'll be setting up gilded cages next."

Slade checked his phone again, then cursed and threw it back into his pocket. Her heart went out to him, but he was doing this to himself.

"Surely he can see that he's driving himself crazy," Cass said. "Jenny is a grown woman. She's going to make her own decisions whether he likes it or not. By not supporting her, he's actually making everything worse."

"Yeah, and Jenny's not happy about it."

"That's not what I mean," Cass said with a little laugh. "I mean, he's destroying his mental health for no good reason, for something he can't change."

"I've never thought of it that way," Flash said. "But I guess you're right."

"You don't have to guess," Cass said firmly.

"He's got to work on this, just like you have to work on your anger."

"Excuse me?" Flash asked.

"You heard me," Cass said gently. "Your anger makes you impulsive. More than that, I know you regret your outbursts. Both of you have issues."

"I have every right to my issues," Flash growled. "I got fucked over."

"So, you take it out on anyone whenever you feel like it?"

"No, I don't. Why are we even talking about this?"

"When you could be talking about me," Slade snapped from behind them. Cassandra whipped around and saw Slade's sullen expression.

"Slade! I didn't realize you were there."

"Obviously. I could see you were right in the middle of a psychological assessment."

Cass frowned. "What, do you deny you need to work on your attachment issues or that Flash has an anger problem?"

"I'm not denying anything," Slade said curtly. "Nor am I confirming anything. We should go."

The two boys turned away from her and stalked toward the checkout register. She had no choice but to follow. She'd been hoping for a nice lunch with the guys, but now that she'd pissed them off, she wondered if they even wanted to talk to her.

She took her time following them, admiring their different characteristics and the way they seemed to scream charisma. She was drawn to them both so strongly she wondered if she would ever be able to walk away from them.

It doesn't matter how strong the magnetism is. This relationship will never have legs.

She laughed softly at her own pun. It was funny, but it was true. These guys were emotionally unstable, and clearly, they had no desire to work on it.

This might just be a bit of fun for a short time. I'm not ready to stop, not yet.

That thought frightened her a little. The smart thing to do would be to jump out of it right now before she became more entangled with them. She already felt like she was in too deep.

I'm going to get hurt, really fucking hurt if I don't look at this objectively. I've got a job to do, and I can't be led astray by two lost boys, no matter how hot they are.

She followed them up to the counter, running lines of good sense through her head like a mantra. The trouble was that her heart and body weren't listening, and there was nothing she could do about it.

Except keep following them, keep having amazing sex ... keep falling in love?

CHAPTER 18

CASSANDRA

Leaving the mall, the two guys were quiet to the point of awkwardness. Cass tried to invite them for food or ice cream, but both just grunted. She was becoming extremely frustrated by their behavior ... surely, they could take a little constructive criticism?

The problem was their reactions immediately made Cass feel like giving up. They were both powerful, complicated, and gorgeous, and she was a difficult woman that was impossible to love.

On the way home, she racked her brain for a way to get the conversation going again and eventually went back to shop talk.

"So, have either of you got a plan for tonight?" she asked, using her toughest professional voice.

"Yeah," Flash muttered. "Find Crenshaw, single him out of the crowd, and interrogate him."

"Might want to go with a bit more finesse, there," Slade said. "Why don't we have a drink with him or something? Just see if we can get him talking?"

"I like that idea," Cass said, trying to give encouragement so the guys would keep talking.

"Why, is my plan too angry?" Flash snapped, taking the bait. Cass sighed.

"If you really want my opinion, maybe it is," Cass snapped right back.

"Honestly, I don't think that dragging the guy into a straight-backed chair is the best way to go," Slade said.

"Yeah, well. You just want to go to see if your sister is there," Flash muttered sullenly.

"Shut your mouth!" Slade yelled, twisting the wheel of the car as he turned to look at Flash. Cass, in the back, was thrown around a little as Slade gained control of the car.

"Who's hungry?" Cass asked. "Come on, I'm starving. Let's go through a drive-thru."

Even though the guys responded with sullen glares, Slade pulled into a fast-food joint. They ordered burgers, fries, and shakes, and then Slade got back on the road toward home.

"Thank you for the dresses," Cass said, trying a new tactic. "It's very sweet of you."

"My pleasure," Slade said. She could tell by how he caught her eye in the rearview mirror that he wasn't just talking about the sex. Buying her pretty things had genuinely given him joy.

"Will you help me pick one out? I'm not sure what to wear."

"I'd love to," Slade said. "But Flash is somewhat of a fashion buff."

"Really?" Cass asked, giggling.

Flash shrugged. "I may admit to having watched a few fashion shows in my time. I'll have a look and help you choose."

"I don't know how formal this gathering is," Cass said thoughtfully. She took a long, hard sip of her vanilla shake. "And I think I should fit in, you know, for the cover."

"Absolutely," Slade agreed. He turned the car onto their street. "We don't want you dressed in red if everyone else is in gray."

"Have you guys got suits?" she asked. Flash laughed.

"Quite a few," he answered. "Luckily, a suit fits

in everywhere."

Slade rolled up the driveway, stopping the car before going into the garage. There was a flurry of activity for a few minutes as they picked up their food and Cass's dresses, then headed inside.

Cass went straight to the living room, settling on the couch as she devoured her fries. She felt like this situation had gotten too emotionally charged, and she needed to manage the guys' expectations on this.

The only reason they reacted the way they did was because they felt like there was too much at stake. I need them to understand it's not going to be like that.

"Hey, guys?" she asked, watching them as they came into the room. "Can you just sit and talk with me for a minute?"

"So long as it's not about my attachment issues," Slade muttered.

"Or my anger management problem," Flash snapped. Cass sighed.

"Guys. That's exactly what I want to talk about. You don't need to stress out about my opinion on anything. I'm not looking for something long-term."

Both of them stared at her in shock. Cassandra took this to be a good sign and plowed on.

"It doesn't matter how good a relationship seems to be. I'm extremely high maintenance," Cass said matter-of-factly. Even though it made her feel bad to admit it, she was also very proud of herself for recognizing her issues and owning up to them.

"High maintenance?" Slade muttered. "What ..."

"No, let me finish," Cass said, on a roll now. "I don't want you guys getting upset about anything I've said. I spoke out of turn ... but since it's not going to be long-term, you don't have to worry about my opinion or what I think. It's just not a big deal."

There was a moment of silence where she could see the guys struggling to speak. It made her feel terrible for complicating their lives. She got up from the couch to stand in front of them in the kitchen, ready to put her foot down.

This is what always happens. I was right to get this out of the way now.

"A long-term relationship just isn't in the cards for me," Cass said. "Something always goes wrong, so I've just let it go. I'm sorry if you got the wrong idea here."

"Wait, wait," Slade said, raising his hands.

"What exactly are you trying to say?"

Cass sighed.

"I got too involved with both of you. Really, it's my fault. It just felt so good to be with you. I let myself get carried away. I feel like it's all getting a bit too serious, but it doesn't have to be."

"Doesn't have to be?" Flash echoed. "You're our fated mate. It doesn't get much more serious than that."

"Exactly," Slade said, frowning. "I don't know where all of this is coming from. Both of us know you feel it. There's no point in denying it."

Cass looked into his eyes, feeling tenderness tugging at her heart. When she switched her gaze to Flash, he had the same expression. It made her want to run to them, hold them tightly, and never stop kissing them. But it would send a bolt of pain through her chest.

"I'm sorry," she said, shaking her head. "I really am. If it was possible for me to have a relationship, I'd move in with you right now, I swear it. But something like that just can't happen for me."

As they absorbed her words, Cass felt a terrible sadness welling inside her. When she was with Slade and Flash, she felt happy in a way she never had. Almost as if she was safe for the first time in her life.

Safe and seen.

As a lump swelled in her throat and tears stung her eyes, Cass begged herself not to cry. It was ridiculous to react in this way when she was doing the best thing for all of them.

The way they make me feel ... it's too much. It can't be real. That kind of comfort and connection I don't deserve.

For a moment, both the men seemed stuck in silent mode. Finally, Flash's face turned six shades of red, and he exploded.

"How can you say these things!" he cried, almost yelling. "After what we've felt between us, how can you tell me you'd just walk away?"

"That's not what I said," Cassandra kept her tone flat, even though tears still threatened her eyes. "There is nothing here. What is there to walk away from?"

"Cassandra!" Flash snapped, taking a step toward her. "This is beyond reason, beyond rational thought. This is the mate bond. Without you, we have nothing."

"Don't be ridiculous," she snapped back. "There are dozens ... in fact, hundreds ... of women better suited to the role of mate than me. Trust me, you don't want any of this."

Flash took another step forward, clearly ready to make a fight out of it. Cass got up on her toes, ready to throw down. The fact he was demonstrating his anger issues only helped her to feel strong in her argument.

"Wait," Slade put a hand on Flash's shoulder. "Just wait."

Flash looked at Slade, his body strung tightly with tension he was desperate to release in a poorly thought-out flood of hurtful words. Cass watched them stare at each other for a second, and Flash seemed to calm down.

"We need to hear her concerns, brother," Slade said, his voice soft and reasonable. "I know we both have a strong feeling about this, but Cass is stating her concerns and boundaries. Only a mad dog would ignore that, right?"

Flash said nothing but growled low in his throat.

"Right?" Slade asked forcefully. Cass saw his hand tighten on Flash's shoulder.

"Right," Flash said, taking a deep breath. Obviously, he didn't agree, but he was going to shut up and listen to Slade.

"I'm not going to argue with you," Slade said gently. "But I would ask that you take a bit more time to think about this if it is your final decision. All of us have had tension running high for a few days, and all of us are strung out. Is it the best time to make a permanent decision?"

"I just don't want you to get your hopes up," Cassandra said softly. "As soon as things get serious, the whole situation implodes. I'd rather not see that happen this time."

Slade nodded. "I understand. But since we have to stay together until the case is done, why not just think about it for now? Once the Crenshaw business is over, then you can decide for good."

Flash glanced at Slade, then back to Cass. He clearly wasn't happy about how the conversation was going, but he didn't say anything. Cass just kept looking into Slade's big, deep eyes, and the emotion she saw there made her feel worse.

The idea of stringing them along, letting them expect things she couldn't possibly deliver, tore her apart inside. The longer they stayed together, the more attached they would all become, and the harder it would be to break up.

But since we have to stick together to nail Cren-

shaw's ass to the wall, there's really not much I can do about it until we unravel the plan.

"Okay," she said, sighing. "I'll wait for now. Once we have Crenshaw sorted, then I'll decide on the terms of our relationship."

The guys seemed satisfied, happily going back to their food. It was almost as if the conversation had never happened. Cass backed away from the counter, turning to the nearby window.

The afternoon was bright, a picture of innocence stolen right from a child's storybook. The gilded rays of the sun and the chirping of small birds did little to cheer her up.

I'm not going to change my mind. How could I? Even if I was relationship material, Flash is a fucking rage machine, and Slade is overprotective to the point of paranoia.

Flash's emotional instability had already upset her, and now that she'd seen Slade have a proper freak out over his sister, she was scared he might try to treat her the same way.

She turned away from the bright scene outside and watched the boys as they joked together. Even though it hurt her heart terribly, she knew this moment could not last.

CHAPTER 19

CASSANDRA

She remained calm as she and Slade pulled up to the party. It was on the fortieth floor of the building, and she'd been told that Flash had arrived earlier and taken his post for the evening. He kept a watch on Edwards while Slade stood next to her, looking focused.

"You in?" Slade asked next to her, giving her his arm to hold onto while entering the building.

"Yes," she heard Flash say from Slade's earpiece, along with soft Halloween music playing in the background. She swallowed, hoping she had shoved her earpiece deep enough in her ear so no one noticed.

Since it was Halloween-themed, everyone

wore whatever they wanted. She and Slade decided to simply wear masks for their outfits before they left. They would blend in just fine.

They walk into the building and up to the fortieth floor, taking in all the Halloween decorations. Ghosts hung from the ceiling, and the food display was quite creative. There was a body where the intestines were the food. Pumpkins were filled with candy, and the drinks were a deep red like blood.

She swallowed and felt Slade's arm tighten on hers, reassuring her. They could do this. They were in and out within an hour easily. They had planned for this.

Her stomach told her there were parts they didn't, and that scared her a little. She didn't like the unknown, and certainly not in this situation. Anything could go wrong.

She scanned the crowd, looking for Crenshaw. He was a powerful demon, and she could feel his energy. Ba'al ... the demon she determined was behind all of this ... possessing Crenshaw was a smart move for the demon, not so much for the human. He had billions of dollars and all the social media viewers he could ever want. It made for a disaster for them.

It wasn't hard to pick him out as he stood by the bar with a couple guards sipping on a glass of wine.

Crenshaw was in his forties with thick glasses and black hair. He looked in good condition, but she could see the demon inside. Henry's features were slightly altered, like the dark circles under his eyes and the way his eyes took everything in.

A woman stood next to him, batting her eyelashes. She was clearly trying to grab his attention, and it worked a little. But he wasn't really giving her attention.

Cass could only wonder if this woman knew who he was and just all the dark and terrible things he'd done. The man wasn't innocent.

Slade released her hand, grabbing them two glasses. He slid one toward her, and she gave him a weak smile.

She ran over the plan in her head once more. They had all discussed it, making sure everyone knew each of their roles. Flash was to keep Edwards occupied so Slade could break into Crenshaw's office. She was to ensure that Crenshaw was distracted during everything. Although neither guy was excited about the idea.

She'd made sure her dress was shorter and

that her neckline dropped. She wore jewelry to pull attention where she wanted it. She was to look like a trophy to catch Crenshaw's attention.

"Are you still holding your station?" Slade asked into his earpiece, giving a smile at a couple that walked past them.

The music grew louder the farther they walked in, and her nerves started to get the better of her. She was used to missions and putting herself in tough positions, but this was different. She wasn't using her brain or her strength to win here. She was using her body.

She straightened her back and looked at Slade when they stopped at the bar. She gave him a smile as he looked at her, squeezing her hand once more.

And just like that, he slipped his hand free and strode across the room. She took a sip of her wine, hoping the liquor would give her a little more courage. She was going to need it.

She could do this. She knew how to do this. And if she didn't, she'd make herself.

She sauntered toward Henry, who was starting on his second glass of wine. His guards watched her with sharp eyes, and she swayed past them, being sure to add an extra swing into her hips. She took a deep breath in as she followed through with her next move.

She dropped her purse, allowing all the content to spill across the ground. Her lipstick and the small perfume bottle, including the condoms that Slade threw into it when they first arrived.

"Oh my god. This is bad." She gasped, bending over quickly to grab everything. She snagged the lipstick, making sure to leave the condoms out for him to see a little longer. "I'm so embarrassed." She looked over her shoulder at Crenshaw and his guards.

The guards looked both disgusted and entertained at her show, but Henry smiled almost as if he'd looked at prey. He pushed himself off his bar stool and bent over, grabbing at the packets of condoms.

She held back a smile, smug about how easy it was for her to grab his attention. Honestly, it was a little gross.

She forced a blush to cover her face and took the condoms, putting them into her purse. "I'm embarrassed. No one was supposed to see that."

Henry chuckled, and she could see the

demonic inside him. His eyes darkened for a split second longer than normal. "What's your name, darling?"

"Lou," she lied, batting her eyes.

He smiled. "Lou, how about I show you a private place so you can organize your purse?"

She gave him a smile, looked across the room, and saw that Slade had made it to the exit. He had to go down to the thirtieth floor for the office.

Henry escorted her down the hallway and opened a door leaving his guards behind. She took in the space with the lush furniture and the smell. She cringed. It was ripe from sex in there. She's not the first girl he'd made his moves on tonight.

"Condoms? Rather bold to bring that to a Halloween party." His voice came out rougher, making goosebumps run down her spine.

"Well, you never know," she said, looking around the room. She wondered if he had anything in here that would be useful. Probably not. This was clearly his sex room.

"I'm in his office," Slade announced through the earpiece.

"How about a drink? Help you relax?"

She looked at him, seeing the way his eyes looked over my body. "Of course."

She wasn't bringing her lips anywhere near that glass. God knew what he put into it.

"So, Lou. You're new to the building, I'll guess."

She nodded while she took a seat on the couch. "Yes, eager to work."

He walked back with two glasses and smirked at her. He handed her a glass, and she took it, holding onto it. He took a sip of his and sat next to her.

She watched as his eyes raked over her body, and her stomach churned. She resisted the urge to vomit and instead smiled. "You must be willing to work hard and climb the ladder."

"Of course," she said with a nod. "This is a big business, and lots of room for me to grow."

He leaned forward, placing his hand on her knee. "I know another way for you to grow quickly."

She swallowed and chuckled. "I see where you are headed, but that would be wrong. You're my boss. I'd rather not get on anyone's bad side on day one."

"Ahh, but it's always best to stay on your boss's good side." He squeezed her knee. "And I like to please in more ways than one."

She sat the glass down. "Sir, it would be wrong."

"I'm leaving the office. I got everything here." Slade spoke up, and she internally smiled. That meant she could get out of this room.

"Cassandra, leave now," Flash said, and she realized he sounded angry. It's possibly because he could hear everything that was going on.

"I really should get back to the party."

She pulled herself up, but he grabbed her arm, pulling her back down. "Lou, we only got started. Come on, just a drink, and it's fine."

She frowned. "No, I'm going to head back to the party now."

His face shifted, and the nice man left. He growled at her. "A girl like you doesn't get to drop condoms on the ground and just walk away. Stop trying to be innocent."

She shoved at him, but he shoved her back, slamming her hard into the couch. She cried out as his hand pressed hard down on her throat, pinning her to the couch. "You're wearing a dress like that and hardly covering any of your skin. You're begging for a fuck at this point. I can practically smell you."

Fear tore at her, and she tried to break free, but his fingers only tightened around her throat. She could only whimper. He pinned her legs, and his hand skated up her thigh. She clawed at him, and suddenly the door busted open.

Slade stepped into the room, looking pissed. He narrowed his eyes on them, and Crenshaw was quick to get up. She gasped for air, rolling herself off the couch.

"Who the fuck are you?" Crenshaw growled out.

Slade almost laughed, shaking his head. "It's over, Crenshaw. We know what you and Edwards are planning."

She coughed, shaking her head. She sucked in a deep breath before she looked up at Crenshaw, seeing he had a hard expression plastered to his face. "I don't know who you are, but I'm going to ask you to leave nicely."

"You and Edwards are planning to have millions of viewers tune in on Halloween to see if they won the five hundred million dollars that you're offering as a cash prize."

She watched as Crenshaw's eyes darkened, and she realized that Slade was stating facts, and

Crenshaw was pissed that he knew. It made her stomach churn, seeing the big picture fall into place.

Slade took another step into the room. "And all of those people that are staring into a screen will be part of a ritual spell that you're doing to release the worst demon of them all, the devil."

If that's the case, everyone was fucked. The entire world would be gone, and most of humanity would die.

A spell like that would need a sacrifice of millions of souls to be completed, but he had that part figured out. Millions of people would tune in to see if they won.

"Aren't you a smart one?" Crenshaw smirked. "So brilliant, aren't you?"

Slade had heard enough and lunged at Crenshaw, who was no longer calm and collected. He allowed his true colors to show and laughed a high-pitched, inhuman cackle, startling Slade. Crenshaw grabbed him around the throat and slammed him to the ground.

"Better luck next time." Crenshaw then lifted her man like a toy doll and threw him across the room and through the forty-story window, glass shattering

Her mouth hung open, and Crenshaw turned to her. His smile was sinister. "You're next."

She took a step back, but she had nowhere to run. She was trapped.

CHAPTER 20

FLASH

The plan was going well. He'd watched Edwards from a distance and stood guard at the back door. Everything was good until Edwards started to move. One moment he was there, and the next, he was gone. Panic filled Flash as Edwards was his only priority.

He left his post and found Edwards heading down the stairs. He was quick on his feet, moving impossibly fast for a human. Flash followed, being sure to stay far enough that Edwards didn't hear him.

Edwards left the building, and Flash had to follow. He couldn't lose him or, worse, miss something that was vital to their mission. He didn't like the idea of being farther from the others, but he didn't have a choice.

Once he was outside, Edwards continued around to the rear employee patio. Then Edwards turned to him, and it was clear he knew he'd been followed. Flash sucked in a deep breath and internally groaned.

Edwards didn't speak. He just shifted into his rhino form and pounded his front hoof into the ground.

"Shit," Flash mumbled as Edwards charged him at full speed. Flash dove to the side, feeling the breeze from the passing rhino.

Edwards snorted as he turned around, shaking his head angrily. He ground his hoof into the grass before springing forward again.

Flash pulled himself to his feet, knowing he wasn't supposed to engage. But damn, it was hard. It was supposed to be easy. This wasn't.

His anger simmered to the top, and he had a hard time keeping it contained. Why did he have to stay in human form and avoid getting his ass beat?

The rhino raced toward him and, this time, hit him. Flash flew backward, slamming into a picnic table for employees to eat lunch outside. It splintered, and the rhino snorted, pleased with himself. It only pissed Flash off more.

The beast ran at him again, and Flash grabbed a part of the table and chucked it at the animal. It hit Edwards on the side of his face, slowing him down and making him veer off to the side, slamming into a tree.

His temper was heating. He could only hope that Cassandra and Slade's part was going smoothly.

"Edwards, give it up," he growled. "We know your plot, and it's not going to work. You are making a big mistake if you try to go through with this."

Edwards snorted and charged, and Flash threw another piece of the table. He wanted to shift and rip the animal apart. He was losing control. How could he not?

This man was part of a plan that would hurt millions of people already hurting. Those depressed and desperate were dangling on fishing lines by these bastards.

Flash didn't know how much blood was already on this demon's hands, but if they went through with their scheme, there would be a hell of a lot more. He couldn't allow that to happen.

Suddenly, something from above slammed into Edwards, smashing him hard into the dirt. The ground shook as Flash lost his footing but caught himself.

A body bounced, landing next to him. He watched Slade roll over with a groan.

What the fuck?

"I had this under control," Flash griped. "You didn't need to fly to the rescue." He threw his hands up. He glanced at Edwards, who was out, which he was grateful for. "Where is Cassandra?"

Slade blinked and looked up at him with a horrified expression. Flash realized Slade hadn't jumped in to help him.

Flash looked up, taking in the glass that was following him and the large hole in a window on the top level. His stomach flipped.

Slade didn't choose to lend his body to help here. From the looks, his ass got pushed out of that window. Flash swallowed and looked at him. This was bad. Cassandra was still in the building alone with Crenshaw.

"What the fuck happened?" he growled, knowing his anger was nothing compared to what it was about to be. If Cassandra was in that building alone, god only knows what would happen to her.

Actually, he knew what would happen to her. He'd lived it and wouldn't wish it upon even the nastiest human beings on the planet. The needles, the mind games, and the drugs that were pumped through his body. He had been in hell.

Slade tried to get up but failed. His legs trembled, and his arms shook. It was understandable why. He just fell out of a building. Correction, he was thrown. Any normal human would be dead. He'd have some bruises in the future.

"Slade! Where is Cassandra? What the fuck happened up there?" He ran his hands through his hair, already envisioning seven different scenarios.

Slade finally pulled himself up. He was about to say something that was going to infuriate Flash.

Slade's eyes wavered. "He caught us off guard. Cassandra had it under control until she didn't. I tried to tackle him, and he threw me out the window. He has Cassandra." He shook his head. "We need to get back in there before it's too late."

Rage filled him, and he wanted to take it out on Slade for a split second. How could he allow this to happen? They had a plan. And even if the plan went wrong, they were never to leave her alone. She was their mate.

But yet, his part didn't work out either, so he couldn't be mad. Correction, he couldn't be mad at his partner.

Flash shifted, his bones snapping and his muscles lengthening. He roared and raced into the building. Slade was behind him, lagging a little. Flash stormed through the doors, and demon-possessed guards glared at them. There had to be at least a dozen of them.

"Shit," Slade muttered behind him.

Guns fired, and they both ducked for cover. The glass shattered, and he glanced at Slade. He looked like shit, but he was shaking it off.

"Top floor," he said, wanting to make sure they both knew where they were headed if they were split up.

He jumped out, ramming the two guys nearest to him. He took them down, disarming them. Blood sprayed all over the white tile, and more shots were fired. He slid behind another pillar.

Slade took his opening, taking out a guard that tried to sneak up behind him. He ground his teeth together. He quickly shifted back into his human form and slid beside Slade.

"We're outnumbered." At this rate, it was going to take them forever to get up to the top floor. Not to mention all the innocent people attending the party. This was turning into a shit show.

"Slade."

They both turned as someone called out. His eyes widened as he watched Jenny come baring down, taking three men in her wake.

Flash was impressed. She knew how to disarm. Slade looked furious to see her here.

"How did you ... when ... why are you here?" he asked, stumbling for the right words. "How did you even know to come here?"

"I have my ways," she said, tucking tighter behind the pillar next to him. "And it looks like you could use an extra hand."

"How did you know to find us here? How did you get in?"

"I snuck in as extra help in the kitchen. When they wanted my ID, I simply said I was late and that if I didn't get in, Crenshaw was going to be pissed. That my bills depend on this job. They took pity."

Smart. She clearly thought her way through this.

"How did you know to come here?" Slade demanded.

"I told you I was investigating things. I have my connections just like you do."

Flash felt appreciative, but it seemed Slade didn't.

His face hardened. "Jenny, it's too dangerous for you here. Why did you even come? You need to go home where it's safe."

Jenny's face fell, and Flash scowled at Slade. "Are you kidding me? This is what Cass was talking about. This is where that overprotective side of you needs to shut the fuck up."

Slade snapped his gaze to him, and he avoided a gunshot. "We need the help, and we need her here. Stop being the overbearing brother and let her spread her wings already."

Jenny looked at him with hope, and Flash stood frozen for a moment. Slade took a deep breath and looked over his shoulder, taking in the scene. They needed the extra hand, and as much as he didn't want to admit it, it was about time he saw Jenny as an adult.

"You know I'm only this way because I never want anything to happen to you." Slade looked back at her. "I want to make sure you are safe because it's what they would have wanted. I'm sorry for treating you like a child."

Jenny gave him a soft smile. "I'm not a little kid anymore, Slade. I can do this. Let me prove that to you."

Slade studied her for a moment before he nodded. "All right."

And just like that, the group grew from a disastrous duo to a team of three. For a moment, he thought they could make it work. Then guards popped out of nowhere, and even with Jenny at their side, they were still outnumbered.

"Where are they coming from?" Slade asked, throwing another man across the room. His screams filled the air, but they were all too busy to care.

"I don't know, but we need to figure something out, or we are screwed."

Jenny was trying to keep up, but they were all falling back. They were pressed to the exit, and he started to worry. What if they couldn't make this work? What if they lost her? What if Crenshaw got what he wanted, and their world was forever changed?

They just might lose.

They were back outside, and the air seemed

bitter now. He felt a storm brewing, and someone smacked Jenny, throwing her sideways. Slade turned to her just as another hit him, knocking him on his ass.

He lost focus, and the side of a gun hit him, throwing him back. His head bounced off the ground, and he tried to shake it off. Fuck.

He looked over the building and took in a hundred guards coming at them. They took down twenty, and thirty more materialized. He didn't see a way of getting out of this.

CHAPTER 21

CASSANDRA

Something cold and hard pressed against Cassandra's cheek. Her entire body ached, especially her joints. She groaned, trying to blink her way back to the conscious world. As she tried to raise her head, a pounding started in her temples that made her feel dizzy and weak.

Just breathe, breathe ... don't try to move too much.

Even though she tried to take her own advice, the cold, hard sensation underneath her was too uncomfortable, and she had to try to get up again. As she placed her hands against the surface and pushed herself up, she realized that she was face down on a concrete floor.

Immediately, her senses began to return to her. The room was very dark, only lit by pale security lights that glowed along the corners of the ceiling. Thick bars surrounded her, too close together for her to slip through.

"You're awake, little lady." The voice was kind and soft, gentle, even. It set her nerves on fire from the insincerity dripping from it.

"Where are you?" she said softly. Cass was trying to sound tough but not doing a very good job.

Laughter echoed around the room, making it impossible for her to determine the direction it came from. As her frustration grew, Cass thrust her hands down and attempted to get up so she could take control of the situation.

As soon as she moved, she heard the clank of chains. It took her a moment to understand what was going on.

I'm chained to the fucking wall.

The chains were loose enough to allow her to rest flat on the floor, but only just. She sat up and looked around, seeing the restraints on her wrists and ankles looped through holes in the wall. As the laughter around her increased, the chains got tighter until she was pressed flat against the concrete.

"I hope you enjoyed your little nap," the gentle

voice came again. "I tried to make you as comfortable as possible."

"Show yourself," she muttered, her eyes darting around the dark corners. She cast her gaze around so fast she almost missed the two very small points of red light. She gasped as she registered them and looked back into the corner where she'd seen them.

Glowing like tiny coals, the two crimson points fixed on her. They disappeared for a second, then came back blazing twice as bright as the creature blinked.

Its feet scratched across the floor as it came toward her. She kept her eyes on the lumbering shadow, her jaw set as she prepared to face her enemy.

It came forward into the pale light. When she finally saw it, she wasn't surprised.

"Crenshaw," she hissed. "Or should I say Ba'al?"

"Correct, my dear," the creature said, bowing its head slightly. "I'm impressed by your efforts, I must say. We could use a woman of your skill on our team."

"No chance," Cass muttered.

"Of course. I expected no less from a demon hunter like yourself."

Even though she knew it was hopeless, she fought the chains and thrashed against the wall. It only made them tighter, and a clunking sound behind her made her feel like there was a mechanism in the wall for tightening them.

Crenshaw approached the bars, his face inhuman in the deep, flickering shadows. All she could see were the red glow of his eyes like rubies with fire behind them and the lines on his face that made up his wide, cruel smile.

"My master loves blood," he whispered. "And pain. Humans are so very useful for that. But you, my dear, will be a very special sacrifice for the dark lord. He will find you very tasty, indeed."

"Fuck you!" Cass screamed, fighting the chains again, only making them tighter.

"Alas, no," the thing chuckled. "It's your blood and pain I want, not your body. Even if it is a lovely one."

Fury rose in her chest, not just for herself but for all the people who were going to die. First, there would be the sacrifices to bring the dark lord to the world, then he would wreak terrible destruction upon the earth. Billions of innocents would die.

Hey, God? If you're up there, you might want to lend us a bit of a hand.

She looked back to the demon, and he had his eyes half closed as he huffed through his nose. The sight of him inhaling her scent made her feel just as violated as if he had actually touched her.

"Beautiful blood," he muttered. "I can't wait to bathe in it. I'll paint the walls with it. I know I won't be able to control myself for long. If I were you, I'd pray for me to lose my mind quickly. Then I'll kill you sooner. If I manage to hold on to my wits ... I could torture you all night."

Cass flexed, ready to fight the chains again, but stopped herself at the last second.

"I will not be your sacrifice," she replied. "And I'm not going to let you hurt anyone."

Crenshaw dipped his head to look through the bars at her. After regarding her for a few seconds, he began to laugh. He laughed so hard that he had to grab the bars of the cell to hold himself up.

"Oh, my dear. I admire your spirit, truly. But how, exactly, do you hope to get away?"

Cassandra struggled for a moment. She had always gotten herself out of even the worst situations by using her wits. No matter how hard she thought about it, she couldn't see a way out of this situation.

No magical gear, no weapons. Tied by ever-tightening chains.

It looked pretty hopeless, but her mind turned to the only place left. It was as if her heart whispered to her that the truth of love would beat the deceit of evil every time.

"My wolves will come for me," Cass said. Her voice was strong with the power of her love. "They won't leave me here to die. Flash and Slade will come, they will rescue me, and they'll tear your sorry ass to shreds when they do it."

Ba'al watched her, an inhuman smile stretching across its face as if it had been cut open by razor blades.

"Why should they come for you?" the thing hissed. "You don't even want them. You told them you didn't love them."

"How do you know that?" Her eyes narrowed on him. "How the fuck do you know anything about me?"

Crenshaw laughed. "I'm sure you know about demons. We can see pain and fear. We can look right into people's hearts. You, my dear, are dripping with fear and pain. You told them it would never work out between you. Tell me, why would they come for you?"

His words hit her with so much force it was as if they were physical weapons that cut straight into her. She tried to stay strong, but fear and loss rose in her, and she sagged against the chains.

I knew it. I knew it. I started to rely on them. I got complacent. I knew I should never have gotten involved with them.

Tears fell as her chin rested against her chest. Crenshaw laughed, and she knew he would wring as much pain out of her as he could before he tortured her to death.

As she closed her eyes and submitted to her horrible fate, she felt warmth growing in her heart. With every beat, strength grew inside her. Cass kept her head down and her eyes closed so the demon wouldn't suspect anything and tried to tune into the feeling to see what it was.

With her eyes shut, trapping her in darkness, visions appeared in the abyss within. She saw horrible demons going down, one after the other. She felt the fists pounding flesh, the blood on knuckles and hands.

Flash?

The vision swirled, and she found herself looking out of Slade's eyes. As well as his physical sensations, she could feel the love and determination in his heart.

They are coming ... they are both coming for me.

Cass fought to control her reaction, not wanting to alert the demon, who was still laughing like a maniac. The contact between her and her mates flickered in and out, but it was undeniable. Her two wolves were fighting to save her, and they were doing it because they loved her.

Completely and unconditionally. I'll never let them go. I've seen into their hearts!

"As fun as this is," Crenshaw said, snapping her attention back to him. "I must be off to begin the ceremony. It's going to be a busy night, and timing is everything."

Ba'al waved as he left the room. Cass watched him go, waiting until she was sure he was gone before focusing on the cuffs that held her.

She knew, now, that all she wanted was to live with her two wolves. Cass could see a future stretching out before her that was full of love and happiness. She would do anything to make that future come to pass.

Finally, I have something worth living for ... something worth fighting for!

With a groan of pain, Cass popped her thumbs out of their sockets so she could slip her hands from the cuffs. She dropped the chains to the floor and wiggled her thumbs back into their joints.

She searched through her hair, praying for lady luck to be on her side. When her fingers found the hard pin at the nape of her neck, she laughed softly, relief flooding her bones. It only took her a few seconds to pick the lock on her ankle cuffs and head to the cell door.

She braced one hand against it and reached through the bars, angling the pin into the lock. Cass was beginning to worry that she would be too late to help her lovers.

That is a demon army out there. No matter how strong my boys are, they are totally outnumbered.

She twisted the pin, fighting the panic rising in her as she thought of her beautiful men being injured in the fight before she could get there. Her chest became tight as her imagination served up a variety of scenes where they could be permanently injured or even killed.

Are they even still alive now? Am I too late?

Suddenly, the door to the cell swung open. Cass jumped back, eyeing it suspiciously.

Doors don't just open.

Glints of red began to wink into existence in the darkness. Shadows lumbered, and feet dragged on the floor. A menacing growl came from the darkness, a sound of pure threat.

Cass took a step back, then another. Suddenly, the main lights switched on right above her head.

Demons!

The room was full of them. All of them were disgustingly ugly, as well as big and powerful. She looked over their ranks in fear, terrified for herself and for her wolves.

Now I'll never get to them in time!

Her next thought was even more hopeless.

No weapons. No gear. Just me, standing here in front of a demon army.

Cass set her chin and glared at the oncoming demons. She planted her feet and raised her fists.

If I'm going down, I'm going down fighting.

CHAPTER 22

FLASH

The fight had been brutal, but Flash, Slade, and Jenny finally managed to cut through the lines of oncoming demons in their attempt to get into the Phar-Scape building.

Flash felt a thin thread of telepathy between himself and Cassandra, and it was shared by Slade. She was in trouble, and he knew they had to get there as fast as they could.

As they approached the lobby of the building, a crowd of possessed humans tore through, heading for the front doors. Slade cursed, urging them back. All of them were brave but not dumb enough to walk straight into a meat grinder.

"What do we do?" Flash asked, looking at the others. "Any ideas?"

"Follow me!" Jenny cried. To Flash's shock, she led them away from the building.

"Jenny, what are you doing?" Slade yelled. "We can't run away."

"We aren't," she said, shaking her head. At the back of the building, Jenny bent down, running her fingers over the edge of a manhole cover.

"Clever," Flash said, winking at the girl. She winked back.

Jenny managed to get her hands under the cover just as the footsteps of the demons pounded toward them from the corner of the building. Before the creatures could see where they were going, all three had slipped into the sewer, and Slade dropped the cover above them.

"Now what, genius?" Flash asked. His voice held respect and warmth. The longer the fight went on, the more impressed he was.

I hope Slade can see her the same way.

When he glanced at his friend, he saw a look of complete admiration on his face, tinged with something like pride. Slade would always worry about his baby sister, but tonight, for the first time, he was seeing her for the incredibly powerful woman she was.

"This way," Jenny said, hurrying through a dark corridor. She whispered under her breath, and Flash realized she was counting her footsteps. After they had gone a short distance, Jenny looked around above them until she found a manhole.

"That one," she said. "It'll take us up to the basement. We should be behind the demon army, and I'm betting that Cass is in the lower holding cells."

"You just know everything, don't you?" Slade said, trying to be sarcastic but clearly impressed. Jenny grinned.

"I was undercover here for quite some time before you guys came in here and junked up my vibe."

"What are you implying?" Slade asked.

"That you're a wrecking machine of incompetence," Jenny muttered, shaking her head.

"Excuse me ..." Slade began, truly outraged now.

"Family bonding later," Flash snapped. "Rescue Cass and foil evil plan now."

Jenny nodded, crouching as she gathered her

muscles, then leapt to grab the manhole cover. She got it open and kicked upward to wriggle through.

"She really is something," Flash muttered, following Jenny and trying to emulate her grace, and ended up smacking his jaw on the edge of the hole.

They waited for Slade to jump through, then hurried out of the storage area where they had come up. Jenny trotted down the hall, her footsteps light as she stayed close to the walls, peeking carefully around each corner. They only ran into a few demons that were easily dispatched.

"You know where you're going?" Slade asked. Jenny nodded.

"Holding cells are just up here."

They turned a corner and approached the doorway, seeing a bright beam of light coming from it. Jenny frowned.

"Looks like it's the only room with all the lights on. I don't know what to make of it."

Slowly, they entered the room. All of them feared a trap, but none of them would back down. Flash paused as he saw the bodies that littered the floor.

"There must be dozens of them," Slade muttered.

"What the fuck went on in here?" Flash asked.

"She's not in the cell," Jenny said.

Flash hurried to the door and looked inside. There was definitely no one there. He turned around, his heart sinking with despair.

Suddenly, a blinding blow struck him on the back of the head. He went down on his knees, shouting out in pain.

"Flash?" a soft voice queried from above.

He looked up, seeing Cassandra unfolding herself from an air duct. She dropped down beside him and wrapped him in her arms. Slade bolted across the room and threw his arms around both of them.

"What happened?" Slade asked, gesturing to the room. "Did you do all of this?"

"Yeah," Cass said. "As soon as I got a break in the onslaught, I hid to regroup. Never expected you guys to come in next."

"Well, we did," Jenny said. "Hello, Cassandra."

"Nice to meet you, Jenny," Cass answered. The two women smiled at each other, sharing a moment of warmth even amidst this chaos.

"Let's get up to the roof and nail this fucker," Jenny said, gesturing to the door.

"Language," Slade muttered.

"Don't even," Jenny muttered.

Cass grinned. "I like this girl."

The two women took the lead, heading for the main stairwell. They headed up, floor by floor, taking out demons as they went. When they reached the penthouse, it felt mostly empty, with a dark aura of black magic emanating from the open area outside.

"This is it," Jenny said. "He's out there."

They paused, all of them trying to think of a plan. As they headed for the outdoor area, a group of people suddenly leapt out from behind a nearby desk and bolted for the elevator.

One of the guys fleeing was a scientist who had personally tortured Flash. "You!" he screamed. Fury bloomed inside him, a terrible rage like nothing he'd ever known.

Without thinking, he turned to the fleeing group and chased them. He'd barely taken two steps before he felt a hand on his arm.

"Flash," Cassandra said, her voice soft. "Stop."

"No!" he screamed, fighting her. "He's getting away. I have to kill him ... I have to!"

"No, Flash," Cass said. "There's no time."

"I don't care," Flash roared, tearing free of her

grip. "He has to die. Do you know what that fucker did to me?"

"No, not entirely," Cass said. "But what I do know is that I need you right now."

Her words penetrated the red haze that swamped his mind. He turned and looked into her beautiful blue eyes, the peace in her gaze like a balm for his wounded soul.

"I need you to stop the ritual. Please, don't give in to your anger," Cass begged.

Flash turned away from her to watch the scientist flee.

I can still catch him if I start running right now.

Flash took a step toward the elevator, almost ready to shift so he could tear the guy to pieces. Cassandra tugged on his arm again, but he didn't look back.

"Flash!" Cass cried. "Please, I need you. I need … my mate."

As the word left her lips, Flash felt a curious feeling cascade through him. It was shock and surprise mixed with an incredible feeling of warmth and intimacy. He turned slowly, falling into her blue eyes all over again.

"Mate?" he whispered. "You need me to be your mate?"

"Yes, Flash," Cassandra said, throwing herself into his arms. "I need you, both of you."

Incredible joy rushed through him as he kissed Cassandra. They were together, really, truly together, and now he knew nothing could ever keep them apart.

"As fun as it is watching you two suck face," Jenny muttered, "are we going to ... like go?"

"Yes," Cass said, stepping away from Flash. "Yes, let's do it."

They approached the glass doors that led out onto the rooftop. Ba'al stood in a circle of blood with symbols drawn inside it. Seven candles ringed the outline.

"No pentagram?" Flash asked, confused.

"Don't get me started on the appropriation of ancient pagan symbols by Christianity," Cass snapped.

"Or the birth of complex writing from sacred geometry," Jenny put in. Flash saw the two women give each other an appreciative look and fist bump.

"Okay, this is what we're going to do," Cass said. "You guys come at him from both sides. He's full of power right now, so he's going to cream you. Jenny, creep around and hit him from the front while he's dealing with the guys. I'll be sneaking up behind him. I literally only need two seconds for the killing blow."

All of them got into position, and Cass waited in the dark shadows by the door. Flash crept around the far side of the roof, watching Slade so they could coordinate their attack.

When they were both in position, they nodded to each other and sprang in perfect time. Their hearts, minds, and even souls in sync.

Ba'al roared as they flew at him, stretching out his hands to hold them in midair.

"You can't stop me," he laughed. "I'm eternal. I'm ..."

Jenny attacked from the front, screaming as she came in with spin kicks. She forced Ba'al back, and his grip on the wolves faltered.

While Ba'al's attention was split, Cass charged from behind, jumping at the demon's back. She clung to his shoulders and held on while he bucked and tried to get free. Flash watched her pull out a long blade she had scavenged from the fight on the way up and cut wildly at Ba'al's neck.

Her third strike sliced his jugular. Hot blood poured out across the circle as the demon screamed, falling to his knees. Flash staggered forward, free of the demon's grip.

"Is it over?" Slade asked.

Cassandra shook her head. "The demon is still here."

Suddenly, she screamed as the demonic presence wrapped around her. Ba'al screamed, too, a disembodied wailing tearing the air as he attempted to crack Cassandra's shields.

"You can't get through!" she yelled, laughing. "You can't possess any of us. We're too strong. But you better do something quick. Crenshaw's body is about to die, and you know what that means."

"Uh," Slade mumbled, "what does that mean?"

"It means," Jenny began with an eye roll, "that if the spirit is in a body when it dies, then it will be trapped and not able to come back."

"Sounds fine to me," Flash said, rubbing his back.

Releasing from Crenshaw's body, Ba'al screamed and whirled around in his demonic form.

"Block your minds," Cass shouted. "Don't let him in."

The air whipped around them like a tornado, stinging and hot. Flash felt like the wind itself was trying to get through the pores in his body. Trying to get inside him, possess him. The only thing he would let take him over was his love for his mate. She was his reason for living, and he would do his best to have her love him.

With his heart full and open … all anger banished, Flash knew the demon would have no power over him. Nothing was stronger than love.

With no body to possess, the demonic presence fled on the back of the fresh night breeze.

Flash ran to his mate, knowing that Slade was right by his side. The only thing both of them wanted was to hold the woman they loved more than life itself.

And never let go.

CHAPTER 23
CASSANDRA

Cass fell to her knees. Now that Ba'al was banished, they no longer needed to fear him.

There were still a few demon-possessed people running around who had to be taken care of. The people with the drug in their systems who had been ready to be brainwashed by Ba'al would also need a couple hours for the medication to pass through their system.

For now, Cassandra couldn't even begin to think of the road ahead. She had never been so exhausted in her entire life. As she sank to the ground, she was sure she was going to collapse, fall flat on her face, and pass out right then and there.

Suddenly, Flash's arms were around her, holding her up. From behind her, she felt Slade's steady grip. Both of the men went down on their knees with her, embracing her from both sides. Slade snuggled against her back, resting his head on her shoulder, while Flash hugged her from the front.

If I wasn't so tired, this could be really hot.

"I love you," Slade whispered in her ear. "I love you so much."

"I love you," Flash said, touching her cheek and looking into her eyes. "I love you more than I've ever loved anything, even my damn self."

Cass laughed softly, realizing tears were flowing down her cheeks. She was relieved and trembling with exhaustion, but her tears were a result of the emotions flooding through her that she couldn't even name.

"I love you," she whispered. "Both of you. I was so afraid ... finding even one person to accept me as I am seemed like too much to ask. To have two? Unbelievable."

Slade wrapped an arm around her waist, nuzzling her neck.

"Believe it," he said. "I'm never letting you go,

Cass. I mean it. I can't stand to be away from you for even a second."

"If you don't believe it, then let us prove it to you," Flash said, kissing her gently. "Every day, I'll prove to you how much I need you in my life and that I'm never letting you go."

Cass leaned back against Slade, and Flash slid forward, so the three of them were pressed up against each other. Cass moaned softly, feeling the incredible thrill of their hard bodies pressed against hers. She had never felt so safe.

"I'm sorry," she whispered, tears still trickling down her cheeks. "I'm sorry I didn't believe and that I said things I didn't really mean. But I love you, both of you, and I can't wait to spend the rest of our lives together."

The guys wrapped their arms around her and squeezed, making her sigh with pleasure. As she relaxed into their embrace, Cass felt a light doze coming on and wondered if they would have to carry her home.

"Hey, guys," Jenny's voice suddenly cracked through the aura of comfort and peace in Cass's mind. "As much as I'm loving you guys grooving on each other, are we going to get out of here, or ..."

Cass laughed softly, looking up but not trying to move.

"I'm in no hurry. You don't have to sit around and wait for us, Jen. You can do whatever you want."

Cass felt Slade's arms tighten as if he wanted to say something, but he simply buried his face deeper in her hair and said nothing.

"I'm pretty wound up, you guys," Jen said. "I don't think I'm done yet. There are still a few possessed guys running around. I think I might go clean up the streets."

"Hey," Slade muttered, trying to look up. "Don't you …"

"What?" Jenny asked with a grin. To Slade's horror, Jenny sat on the barrier along the rooftop and gave him a cheeky wave before dropping over the edge.

"What the fuck?" Slade snapped, getting up. Cass and Flash laughed.

"Did you see that?" Slade yelled. Cass nodded.

"She tied off before she jumped. Look at the corner rail." Cass said, pointing. Slade followed her gaze and saw the glint of a grappling hook and a tough, braided line. The tension went out of it, and the hook disappeared over the edge.

"That kid …" Slade screamed.

"Is fucking amazing," Flash finished.

Cass rocked back into Flash's arms, wondering if it would be okay to just fall asleep and let the guys take her home. Whether it was okay or not, she felt herself slipping away, and for the first time in her life, she had no fear.

She was safe and loved. She would never have to watch her own back ever again.

For the next few days, all three of them lay around in bed, eating, resting, and making love. Cass needed lots of time to recover, and the boys didn't mind waiting on her hand and foot. They decided rather quickly that they wanted to make it official and set a date for the wedding.

Cass didn't want a church or special venue, so they chose a nature reserve in upstate New York that was easily accessible by the rest of Slade and Flash's pack.

She invited her family, doing so with a heavy dose of anxiety. Her parents didn't seem happy about the news she was marrying a wolf shifter … let alone two … but promised to be on their best behavior.

The day of the wedding dawned bright and clear, the sunshine so golden, it looked like pure magic. Mountains rose around the valley against the perfect blue sky, and the trees sang a cheerful serenade as the breeze blew through their leaves.

Cass wore a simple peasant-style white gown and a garland of white rose buds. When she took her first step down the aisle, she was slightly nervous at being sandwiched between her family of demon hunters and a massive, savage-looking wolf pack. Even though her guys and immediate family were in tuxedos, some of the wolves had literally crawled out of the forest with only the fur on their backs.

Jenny waited by the podium as Cass's maid of honor, her cheeks pink with excitement as she welcomed her new sister to the family. She took the bouquet and stepped back so Slade and Flash could take their places on either side of her.

The celebrant was a kindly old woman chosen by Cass's parents. The woman was a master of magic, and in addition to wielding great supernatural forces, she was also certified to perform legal marriages.

The ceremony was brief. Cass had wanted to stay far away from long, sober speeches and drawn out traditional vows. She and the boys had already decided what to say, and the celebrant only had to guide them through.

When the final words "you may kiss the bride" were uttered, Cass reached for both of her men, and they kissed her at exactly the same time on opposite cheeks. Jenny snapped a few photos as the three of them got tangled in each other's arms.

They moved straight to the buffet tables and the small area that had been cleared for dancing. At first, the three of them stayed together to greet members of both families, only drifting apart as the reception got underway.

Cass wandered around the edge of the dance floor, pleased to see her uppity demon-hunting family getting on well with a bunch of "heathen" wood wolves. She knew there would be some obligatory protesting by the more traditional members of her family, but for the most part, everyone looked happy for her.

Not as happy as I am for myself.

Cass smiled as she circled the buffet table, still checking out her guests and making sure they were all having a great time. She had never been so happy, and she knew it was shining through her, an aura of love that could be felt as well as seen.

Now, when I fight, I have something to fight for.

She rounded the table where drinks were being handed out and noticed Slade talking to Jenny. She hurried to get closer and eavesdrop a little, ready to step in if Slade got overprotective.

What she heard shocked her to the bone.

"I'm proud of you, sis," Slade said, giving her a tap on the shoulder. "I didn't realize that I was hurting you by trying to keep you safe. I'm going to give you all the space you need, but please, check in with me every now and then, okay?"

"You got it," Jenny said, grinning. "I'm liking the new attitude, bro."

"Thanks. It's got a lot to do with Cass. She showed me I can love someone and fear for them … while letting them live their own lives and decide what risks they want to take for themselves."

"I'm relieved," Jenny said, laughing. "I can finally go on that lava rafting trip I've been planning."

Slade laughed. "I really hope that you're joking. I'm not sure, though. I have this really weird feeling that if you wanted to do it, you'd nail it. Those were some swift moves that night out against Phar-Scape, by the way."

"I know, right? Did you see me take the head off that demon spawn dude?"

"I did," Slade muttered. "And I was very uncomfortable with the level of violence."

Jenny laughed, leaning in to hug her brother.

"At least you know I can take care of myself," she said.

"That rooftop exit was fucking amazing, too," Slade called after her.

"Of course!" Jenny shot back. "You should see what I can do with a bow and arrow."

"Please, no," Slade muttered. Cass came forward, putting her arms around him.

"Do you need saving, my love?" she asked.

"I do. I'm traumatized. My sister is a blood-thirsty, violent demon killer, and here I was thinking she needed a pony for Christmas."

"She's nineteen, Slade," Cass said with a wry smile. "I'm pretty sure it's not ponies she wants to be riding."

"Please, no," Slade moaned. "I do not need to think about my sister dating."

"Who said anything about dating?" Cass asked, laughing. "I'm sure she just wants to get out and have fun at her age."

"If you do not stop, I am going to pass out from

stress," Slade muttered, taking Cass's hands. She started to sway, leading him toward the dancers flitting around the open glade.

"Not the best time to tell you that I saw her flirting with my cousin Nathan then?" Cass said with an evil grin.

"No," Slade said, his voice pained. "Is he a good guy?"

Cass shrugged. "He's twenty, devastatingly gorgeous, arrogant to a fault, and completely full of himself."

"Thank you very much," Slade muttered. Cass laughed.

"What? Obviously, Jenny likes a challenge. I'm sure she'll rein him in before breakfast tomorrow."

"Stop with the pony analogy," Slade whispered. "And do not even hint that they'll be sharing breakfast tomorrow."

"Okay," Cass said gently. She took Slade in her arms, feeling incredible tenderness for him. He was struggling, but he was still determined to give Jenny her space, and that meant a lot to her.

"I'm proud of you," she whispered, kissing him.

"Why, what did he do now?" Flash's voice said.

Cass jumped as Flash put his hands on her shoulders.

"Where did you come from?" Cass asked. Flash put his arms around her waist and pulled her against him.

"I'm sneaky. I sneaky-stalked you."

"Hmm. Can't say I mind having you behind me," Cass said, smiling.

"I don't mind it either," Flash said, grinning. He reached past Slade to grab Cass's hands.

"Shall we dance?" Flash asked.

Slade grinned. "I'll be back for my turn."

Cass turned to face Flash, melting into his arms as they began to sway together. The breeze sang in the trees around them, and the sky stretched out above her, as endless and deep as her love.

CHAPTER 24

FLASH

The sounds of the reception faded behind him as he hurried into the trees. Some of Cass's family and the wolves were camping out in the forest. Others had rented cabins nearby. Flash had wondered if anyone would actually need their beds, though. It was past midnight, and the party was still going strong.

Flash picked up his pace, wanting to get to his destination before Slade and Cass arrived. He'd set up this surprise much earlier in the day, and he wanted everything to be perfect. As he came through the trees to the meadow, he was pleased to see everything was still and quiet.

A large tent had been set up, the walls glowing

with orange fire from the battery-powered lamps inside. The entire space in the tent was covered in thick pillows and blankets. Champagne and all of Cass's favorite foods waited inside.

He stripped, getting completely naked and throwing himself down on the silk cushions. He was just in time as only a few seconds passed before he heard Slade leading Cass through the forest toward the tent.

"Seriously, where are we going?" Cass said, giggling. "My uncle Elroy challenged your great-uncle Dane to an arm-wrestling contest, and Aunt Celia says a wolf can't beat a mage, but Flash's great-aunt Mabel says a wolf always tops a wizard …"

"I agree, that might be something worth seeing," Slade said, cutting her off. "But this can't wait another second. From the way our families are getting along, I think you might see a few more gatherings like this. Maybe even weddings."

"That'll be the day," Cass muttered. "Oh, what's this?" she cried, surprised.

Flash listened to their steps rustling closer and posed dramatically. Cass threw open the side curtain and burst out laughing when she saw his affected pose, stretched limbs, and overly flexed muscles.

Flash held it for as long as he could before falling down on the cushions, laughing until he was breathless. Cass tried to hurry over to him but tripped on her gown and tumbled down onto the cushions, giggling as Flash caught her.

They rolled across the cushions together until Flash came out on top, pinning Cass by her wrists. He kissed her softly, feeling the heat rising in his body as well as hers.

"Is this your big surprise?" Cass asked. Flash nodded.

"That's why we told you not to book anything for the honeymoon straight after the wedding. We want to hang out in the woods for a while."

"I can get down with that," Cass said, relaxing underneath Flash. "Especially if it's going to be this comfortable. This is like a sultan's tent."

"Good," Slade said, sitting next to her. "That's exactly what we were going for."

Cass giggled as she realized he was naked, letting her eyes linger on his body. Slade's beautiful muscles and smooth skin gleamed in the flickering light, and Flash saw him flex for her.

Not to be outdone, Flash bent his head and

kissed her, kneading her lips with his. He felt Cass soften under him, her legs opening to trap him between her thighs and in the folds of her dress.

"This is the surprise that couldn't wait?" she asked. He grinned, nodding.

"I know I can't wait anymore," he said.

"Neither can I," Slade whispered.

Flash sat up, holding Cass's hands to bring her with him. She settled on her knees, her hands going to the laces on her dress. Flash pushed her hands out of the way.

"Allow me, my lady," he said, his swift fingers moving across the fastenings.

"Hmm, being undressed like a medieval royal. I could get used to this."

"You better," Slade said, leaning over her shoulder. "Because this is how it's going to be for the rest of your life."

Flash watched Slade push the sleeves of the dress off Cass's shoulders, catching the front so he could tug it down around her waist. For a moment, all Flash could do was watch as Cass leaned back against Slade and his best friend's hands wrapped around her waist, coming up to squeeze her breasts.

Cass turned her head to kiss Slade over her

shoulder, turning back to reach out her arms and beckon Flash. He shuffled forward on his knees, cupping her cheek in his hand as he pressed his lips to hers.

His hands passed over Slade's as they went around her waist. Flash felt her hot lips on his, moaning as he leaned toward her, trapping Cass between him and his best friend. She writhed between them, her arousal getting stronger by the second. Flash ached for her and for the final completion of the mate bond ... the claiming bite.

He knew they couldn't rush into the moment, that it had to build until Cass was ready, but he couldn't hold back his eagerness. When he met Slade's eyes over Cass's shoulder, he knew his brother was thinking the exact same thing.

Their hearts and their bodies were in sync in a way they had never been, and it was because both of them were tuned to the needs of their mate more than anything else in the world.

CHAPTER 25

SLADE

Cass's warm body pressed tightly against his. The firm swell of her ass was covered by the soft, white fabric of her dress, but her upper half was bare. He kissed her shoulder and ran his hands along her chest until he could cup her breasts in his palms.

She moaned, leaning back against him. Slade put more pressure on his hands and pulled her even farther back, making Flash grab her hips and stretch her legs out to either side of him.

"Hmm, does anyone mind if I just float and enjoy this?" Cass whispered.

"Mind?" Slade asked. "Of course, we don't mind."

"I wouldn't want you guys to think I was

falling asleep on you," she said with a grin. Flash pulled the dress off her legs, running his hands along her thighs to hook her underwear and tear it off.

"Sleep?" Flash said as he leaned over, his mouth hovering above her pussy. "Who said anything about sleep?"

He dug his hands into Cass's thighs, opening his mouth and sinking his tongue into her pussy. Cass moaned, writhing as her hands clawed at the soft cushions underneath her.

Slade watched his friend pleasuring her, holding Cass gently on his lap. He stroked her collarbone with the tips of his fingers and trailed featherlight touches across her breasts and ribs.

As Cass began to writhe and thrash under Flash's attention, Slade increased his efforts. He rubbed her breasts hard, squeezing them and pinching her nipples. She cried out, bucking her hips up and down. Flash growled and wrapped an arm even more tightly around her thigh as Cass shivered, throbbing under the force of her climax.

"Slade," she whispered, looking up at him. "Please, put your cock in my mouth."

Slade moaned, his voice ending in a strangled gasp. Cass nodded, encouraging him. As he slipped out from under her, Flash kept up the pressure with his lips and tongue, making Cass cry out as he brought her to orgasm again.

Slade knelt by Cass's shoulder, his cock hard and throbbing as he anticipated what was coming next. Lust charged through him, and the savagery of his wolf felt like it was tearing through his blood, ripping his humanity and his control to shreds.

Still, he waited, holding himself still. He was at her command, not his own.

"Yes," Cass murmured, reaching for him. "Yes, Slade. Come here."

Slade leaned forward until Cassandra could reach him with her mouth. When she wrapped her soft lips around the head of his cock he cried out, pleasure streaking through him. The desire to take her increased tenfold, but he maintained control, waiting for her direction.

With a low growl of need, Cass reached out and grabbed Slade's hips, tugging him toward her. He almost fell, managing to catch himself on his hands at the last second as his knees came down on either side of Cass's head.

Slade cried out as she swallowed his cock, her hot, delicate lips wrapping around the base while she sucked the length of him down her throat. Her hands gripped his ass cheeks so hard that her nails pierced his skin. All he could do was hold himself up with his hands and rock gently back and forth with his hips to the pace Cass set for him.

When she suddenly wiggled and screamed under him, Slade tried to pull away, but she dug her nails into him and forced his cock back down her throat. Behind him, he heard Flash moaning as he pleasured Cass with his tongue.

"Come for me," Flash murmured. "Come for me, Cass."

Cass grabbed Slade so hard that he snapped upright, looking to the sky as she twisted under him, forcing his cock down her throat. She writhed as she came, marking him with her nails as she thrashed. As Flash sat up and moved back, Slade gently pulled away, gasping as Cass's lips grabbed at him, teasing him with her tongue.

Slade took a moment to get himself under control, breathing hard and trembling. When Cass smiled up at him, he stroked her cheek and kissed her softly.

"Feeling good?" he said softly.

"Really good," she answered.

"I think I need to get up top," Flash said, his

voice strained. "I almost died watching that action. My cock is about four times bigger than it usually is."

"Oh, really?" Cass asked, winking at him. "You'd better get it up here and put it in my mouth, then."

Flash moaned as if he'd been punched in the gut. He crawled out from between Cass's legs and ran a hand along her body as he slowly made his way up to her mouth. Slade watched them kiss, feeling arousal and tenderness collide inside him, turning into a new emotion that redefined love itself.

"Hey, you," Cass whispered, beckoning him closer with a finger. Slade bent toward her, stealing a kiss from Flash.

"You need to get down below," Cass whispered. "And give me your cock."

Slade kissed her once more, then sat back to watch Flash settle across her shoulders. Slade ran his hands over Cass's belly and thighs, teasing himself as he lowered his mouth to her pussy. As he sucked on her clit, he heard her try to moan, but it was muffled by Flash's cock.

He teased her with his lips and tongue for a few minutes, enjoying the taste and scent of her before sitting up and pressing the head of his cock to her slick pussy.

Even with her shoulders trapped by Flash's legs, Cass thrashed under him, pointing her hips up. Slade ran one finger along her lower lips, making her shiver. Then he teased her with the head of his cock before finally grabbing her hips and sliding himself into her in one long, hard stroke.

Cass went still under them as if her entire body was overloaded with sensation. Then, her pussy clamped around his cock so hard that he gasped, losing his breath. When Flash did the same thing, Slade knew that her lips had trapped his friend the same way her pussy had grabbed him.

Cassandra moaned around Flash's cock, thrashing, and writhing. Slade felt her convulsing deep inside as rivers of come dripped around his cock and down her thighs. He knew that the love of his life was having the best orgasm she'd ever had, stretched, and shared between him and his best friend.

And the night is still young yet. I'm nowhere near done ... and neither is Flash.

CHAPTER 26
CASSANDRA

Cass stretched out between Flash and Slade. Flash's heavy weight across her shoulders and his cock down her throat made her feel needed and wanted in a way she had never dreamed possible.

Slade's cock thrust into her pussy in long, slow strokes. She'd already come so many times that her deeper folds were flushed and slick, but the sensations piling up on top of each other only shattered her nervous system into more powerful spasms.

She leaned her head back, letting Flash pleasure himself on her lips. She wanted to taste him, but she was pretty sure the guys were saving themselves for the big finish.

The claiming bite.

Cass knew it was coming. Now that they had accepted their future together, the wolves had to mark her with their fangs to claim ownership of her. It would be done at the height of passion, so she'd barely feel it.

She wasn't worried about the pain, though. In her years of demon hunting, she had more than likely suffered far worse. She was worried about letting down these two amazing, powerful, and sensitive men. Somewhere deep inside, she'd probably always have a wound that cried quietly, telling her she was unworthy.

Feeling both of the men pleasuring her with such focused attention went a long way to silencing that cry. She wrapped her arms around Flash's ass, sucking him down her throat as Slade began to pound her pussy with hard, short strokes. Another orgasm flooded through her, and thought was forcefully ripped from her mind.

The only thing that was real was the throbbing of her body and the singing of her skin. She rolled back and forth, gasping and shivering. It took her a few moments to realize that both of the men had stopped touching her.

As the tremors began to subside, she looked

up, blinking under the soft glow of the surrounding light. Cass saw the two men sitting on either side of her, just watching her writhe and gasp.

"Hmm, why did you stop?" she whispered.

Flash grinned, shaking his head. "I'm not sure what happened, but it looked to me like your body got overloaded," he said. "I thought a little break was in order."

Slade leaned over, touching her cheek gently. "I'm not sure what happened, either, but it was amazing to watch."

Cass giggled, stretching out on the silken cushions. Her throat hurt, and she was thirsty, but she didn't get a chance to ask before Flash turned away and turned back around with both water and champagne.

"Which would you like?" he asked.

"A sip of both," she said. "How did you know I was thirsty?"

"Aside from an educated guess, the mate bond," Slade said.

He tapped his temple and winked as she drank. Cass waited for Flash to put the drinks aside as she thought about the mate bond.

"You can hear my thoughts?" Cass asked. She

remembered the battle in the depths of the Phar-Scape building and how she'd seen and felt her wolves fighting for her.

"Not really," Flash said. "We can see what you see or feel what you feel. It's a little chaotic right now, but that will change after the claiming bite."

"Yes," Slade agreed. "It will be much clearer."

Cass felt a shiver of anxiety run up her spine. The hint of fear just made every sensation twice as sharp and ten times as intense.

"Show me," she whispered. "Show me exactly what you mean."

Slade shuffled across the cushions to kneel in front of her. He smiled, resting his hands on his thighs with palms up.

"Do you want us to take over?" he asked.

Flash gently touched her shoulders from behind, caressing her with his fingertips.

"Do you trust us?" he whispered.

"Yes," she answered automatically. A swirl of images swam through her head, and Cass had to think about what she was agreeing to for a moment.

She looked up into Slade's eyes, then over her shoulder at Flash. The love she felt for them destroyed any doubts or fears she might have had over what they were about to do. There was only love, comfort, and safety here.

"Yes," she said again, smiling up at Slade. He still knelt before her, his hands on his knees. He smiled back, raising his hands to touch her thighs.

"Close your eyes," Slade whispered.

Cass did, feeling Flash tracing her shoulders with his fingers while Slade touched her thighs.

"Feel me," Slade whispered.

"And me," Flash said.

Cass gasped as the sensations in her body changed. She could feel the rough fingertips of the men on her body. With her eyes closed, the feeling was particularly intense, but there was more, much more.

Somehow, she could feel her own skin under the hands of her lovers. Her mind seemed to split into a three-way consciousness that opened her perception. As the feeling expanded, she expected it to hurt or become confusing, but it didn't.

Slade ran his hands up her thighs, applying pressure with his fingers. Behind her, Flash ran his hands down her back. Cass sat up a little, bracing her knees and opening her legs.

The wordless communication stretched between them, something elastic and alive. Cass felt her own body throbbing with arousal as the two men trapped her between her bodies, but she could also feel her own soft, delicate form as they pressed against her.

For a few moments, the boys rocked back and forth, lulling her. Cass dropped her head to Slade's shoulder, her hands loosely clasped on his upper arms.

Flash bent his head to rest against the back of her neck, gently touching her shoulders. Cass drifted, feeling intense desire rising in her pussy, and feeling the arousal of the men getting stronger as they pressed their hard cocks against her.

Slade shifted, lowering his hips and reaching between her legs. She gasped and struggled instinctively, feeling his hard fingers rubbing her and also being aware of his excitement as he pushed through her hot, wet folds.

She leaned back against Flash, and he grabbed her hip, sliding his hand down to squeeze her ass. She jumped between them, crying out as she realized she couldn't move and that she was now completely trapped.

A moment of fear rose within her. No matter her fantasies, this was real now, really real. Cass realized she was holding her breath and let it out in a soft sob.

Slade stroked her hair. Flash rubbed her arms. They had felt her fear and were giving her their love and their gentleness.

"You're safe," Flash whispered in her ear.

"We'll never, ever hurt you," Slade said softly.

Cass relaxed, feeling the truth of their words. There was still a hiss of danger in the air, and Cass knew it was because the wolves inside her men were about to be let loose and run free.

All over me.

The fear intensified, but so did her desire. Cass opened her legs, bracing her hands on Slade's shoulders as she threw her head back. A soft moan came from Slade's throat that was immediately echoed by Flash as if their bodies were truly connected.

Slade reached down between her legs, shoving his hips up as his other hand pressed down on her shoulder. Cass moaned, squirming as Slade's cock slid into her.

She felt herself slip down, and Slade's cock bumped against her cervix, making her throb and spasm against him. While she was still processing her pleasure ... and Slade's ... she felt Flash getting ready behind her.

He pushed her forward so that her head fell across Slade's shoulder. Flash was the more emotional of the two, and it was obvious that his wolf was running wild in his blood. She could feel his intense arousal, his savagery, and his need.

One of his hands gripped her hip, and Slade covered it with his own. She whimpered, climbing Slade a little as Flash fumbled with his fingers between her ass and his cock.

Slade kissed her cheek, whispering in her ear.

"Beautiful woman. Brave, beautiful woman."

She leaned her head back and kissed him, their lips and tongues slickly sliding together. Her body spasmed around Slade's cock, clenching tight around his hardness with so much force it hurt.

I'm so full ... I can't take any more.

Flash rammed his cock into her ass with one extremely hard, fast stroke. Cass screamed into Slade's mouth, writhing and thrashing between them. The two men stayed still, both of them holding their hips thrust upward to pin her between them.

Cass could feel Flash's hard body pressed against her back, his hands on her shoulders.

Slade's chest rubbed against her breasts, and his hands grabbed her waist. The men stayed completely still for a few moments as she struggled and writhed, overrun by sensation.

Slowly, the tension bled out of her, and she fell against Slade's shoulder, whimpering softly. Her pussy throbbed, an incredible arousal running through her blood. She could feel it coming from both of the men but also someplace deep inside.

Maybe, the deepest darkest place in my soul. The place where I am a very, very bad girl.

Fuck me!

"Fuck me," she whispered, barely able to speak. "Fuck me hard."

Flash groaned, grabbing her shoulder with one hand and her hip with the other. He started thrashing her immediately, thrusting his hard, thick cock into her ass over and over again.

On her other side, Slade stayed still, bracing her against Flash's onslaught. As his friend settled into a more even rhythm, Slade tightened his grip on her waist and began to thrust in slow, short strokes.

The two men fell into perfect sync, and Cass felt that magical resonance in the air that meant all of them were connected. She was completely drunk on the pleasure of being filled, stretched, pounded, and adored from every angle, but she felt the intensity of their pleasure too.

There was a primal, intense driving force behind Flash, tempered by a stable, steady strength that emanated from Slade. Their energy joined around her, threading with her own.

As her heart quickened, the men increased their pace. Cass went limp in their arms, letting them toss her back and forth. A long, low wail built in her throat, and Cassandra closed her eyes, giving herself to the slippery sensations of sweat-slicked skin, the rough, hard thrusts, and the throbbing deep inside that built toward their climax.

She cried out, almost sobbing as she felt both of their cocks thicken at exactly the same time. Flash grunted, crying out, and Slade moaned a long, drawn-out sound. They all waited right on the edge of the peak.

The primal force broke free. She felt while it obliterated the human minds of her lovers. There was only hunger now and the desire for blood.

Slade's teeth clamped onto her left shoulder, and Flash's on her right. She screamed for real, struggling between them as their fangs sank in deep. The men shuddered with ecstasy for a few seconds as blood ran around their teeth and trickled down their throats.

Cass screamed, throwing her head back as the orgasm exploded inside of her. She felt her pussy pounding so hard that her head swam, and she couldn't see. Both of the men cried out at the same time, and she came again as she felt their cocks spurting and shivering deep inside her.

When she fell, they caught her. Cass sank down onto the cushions, murmuring nonsense as she tried desperately to get her breath back. They reached for her, wrapping her in their strong arms and rocking her, soothing her into a relaxed and peaceful stupor.

Darkness wrapped its great wings around her, a shadow of her old fears rising somewhere behind it, but Cassandra was not afraid anymore. She smiled, reaching out for her men, and feeling them hold her even more tightly.

I am loved.

I am seen.

I am safe.

ABOUT THE AUTHOR

New York Times and USA Today Bestselling Author

Hi! I'm Milly Taiden. I love to write sexy stories featuring fun, sassy heroines with curves and growly alpha males with fur. My books are a great way to satisfy your craving for paranormal romance with action, humor, suspense and happily ever afters.

I live in Florida with my hubby, our son, and our fur babies: Speedy, Stormy and Teddy. I have a serious addiction to chocolate and cake.

I love to meet new readers, so come sign up for my newsletter and check out my Facebook page. We always have lots of fun stuff going on there.

SIGN UP FOR MILLY'S NEWSLETTER FOR LATEST NEWS!

http://eepurl.com/pt9q1

Also by Milly Taiden

Find out more about Milly Taiden here:

Email: millytaiden@gmail.com

Website: http://www.millytaiden.com

Facebook: http://www.facebook.com/millytaidenpage

Twitter: https://www.twitter.com/millytaiden

You can find a complete list of all my books by series and reading order at my website: millytaiden.com